A
Harlequin
Romance

OTHER
Harlequin Romances
by ANNE WEALE

LORD
OF THE SIERRAS

by

ANNE WEALE

HARLEQUIN BOOKS   TORONTO
WINNIPEG

Original hard cover editon published in 1974
by Mills & Boon Limited.

© Anne Weale 1974

SBN 373-01848-7

Harlequin edition published January 1975

Printed in Canada

Hill-song of Bores

A girl from Bores, down by La Lama, made me in love.

I thought that love had forgotten me, as one who had long since ceased to have those pains that burn lovers worse than a flame.

But I saw that beauty, so lovely to look at, with a pleasant face as fresh as a rose, and with such a complexion as I have never seen, gentlemen, in a lady or n any woman.

MARQUÉS DE SANTILLANA

THE PENGUIN BOOK OF SPANISH VERSE
trans. J. M. Cohen. Copyright © J. M. Cohen,
1956, 1960. Reprinted by permission of
Penguin Books Ltd.

CHAPTER ONE

IN the summer of her seventeenth year, when she had finished her schooling but was still undecided about her future, Sophie Lingwood was kissed by a stranger in the basement of a secondhand bookshop.

It happened shortly after she had glanced at her watch and discovered, with a gasp of dismay, that she had been browsing for nearly an hour, although she had not meant to linger for more than ten minutes. It was Monday and, unexpectedly, Grandplum was having an American librarian to lunch. What was left of yesterday's chicken was not enough to go round, and Sophie had been sent to the butcher to pick up a parcel of chops. Now, unless she cycled like the wind, the visitor would arrive at Cliff Court before she did.

Replacing *A Lady's Travels Round the World*, the book which had caused her to lose track of time, and snatching up the basket containing the chops, Sophie ran.

The basement of Bramfield's Bookshop was a labyrinth of narrow aisles between floor-to-ceiling shelves of close-packed volumes. As she whirled out of the aisle marked Topography/Travel/National History, a man was emerging from Philosophy/Theology. Had he been one of the elderly clerics who frequented that section of the basement, her onslaught would have sent him staggering.

But as this man was young, much taller than Sophie, and possessed of swift reactions, he was able to shoot out his hands and catch her by the shoulders, reducing the force of her impact against his chest.

Startled, embarrassed, and impatient of any delay, she

stammered an apology. For an instant she had an impression of amused grey eyes in a dark, rather foreign-looking face; and then, instead of relaxing his grip and standing aside for her to pass him, the stranger bent his head and kissed her.

It was only a quick, light kiss, but it was far more shocking than their collision. She could not believe it had happened to her. For several moments she was too dumbfounded to move or utter. At length, when it seemed the stranger was going to say something, Sophie recovered her faculties, pushed past him, and fled

Her heart was still thudding when she burst into the kitchen at Cliff Court, but Mrs. Steel was too concerned about lunch to notice Sophie's agitation. It was not unusual for her niece to be flushed and breathless after pedalling vigorously up the steep hill from the shopping centre.

Sophie had been born in Taiping, in north Malaya (as it then was) during the State of Emergency in the early 'fifties. Five months later, her mother and her soldier father had been shot in a terrorist ambush. Fortunately she had had a grandfather and an aunt to take the place of her parents. Now, hearing from her school friends about the frequent rows they had with their elders, Sophie wondered sometimes if she would have been as happy with her parents as she was with Aunt Rose and dear old Grandplum.

Until his retirement, her grandfather had been a solicitor. But from boyhood his deepest interest in life had been the collection of rare books. The joy of his old age had been to see his grandchild developing the same interest.

Sophie's aunt, Rose Steel, was a professional embroiderer. Widowed on the fateful sixth of June, 1944, while still in her early twenties, she had never met anyone else she wanted to marry, but had found a different form of fulfilment in creating magnificent modern embroideries for

8

churches and public buildings, and in bringing up her younger brother's child.

Sometimes, when her married friends complained that they were continually at odds with their teenage daughters, Rose wondered why she never had trouble with Sophie. From the day when Rose and her father had travelled to Southampton to meet the troopship on which an Army nursing Sister was in charge of the orphaned infant, Sophie had brought them nothing but interest and amusement. The plump, placid baby had grown into a cheerful, loving little girl, content to spend hours watching the passing shipping through Grandplum's telescope, collecting pebbles on the beach, or sewing potholders and egg-cosies from the scraps left over from Rose's work.

By the time she reached adolescence, Sophie was hooked on book collecting. The postman came early to Cliff Court, and breakfast was a silent meal. Rose read the local paper, Mr. Lingwood studied the elegantly printed catalogues put out by Dawsons of Pall Mall, Maggs Brothers, Sotheran's and other leading antiquarian booksellers, and Sophie pored over the titles offered in Wrigley's Greenlist, Jabez Elliott's monthly Miscellany, and the For Sale columns of *Bookdealer*.

Although she was no trouble at home, she had never done very well at school. Her reports had been scattered with disapproving exclamation marks.

Careless! Untidy! Lacks team spirit. Lacks concentration. Must overcome her weakness for wool-gathering!

"Dear me, day-dreaming again, Sophie?" Mr. Lingwood would remark, on reading this last recurring criticism.

"I'm sorry, Grandplum. I do *try* to pay attention, honestly. But Miss Stradbroke makes history so boring. According to her, Lord Bothwell was an absolute villain. I think he must have been super."

"Miss Stradbroke is too much of a realist, and you are too romantic," said her grandfather, with a sympathetic twinkle. "However, I expect you will outgrow it."

But Sophie did not outgrow it. From the age of twelve, until well past her sixteenth birthday, her life was a succession of desperate love affairs with long-dead heroes. While her contemporaries pinned up pictures of pop singers, Sophie's fantasies featured El Gran Capitán, followed by François de Guise, followed by the bad Lord Byron. When her school friends began to feel less enthusiasm for unattainable heart-throbs, and to take more interest in each other's brothers and in the young, dark-eyed Spanish waiters at the town's largest hotels, Sophie continued to find men in books more exciting than Jane Pulham's chinless elder brother, or the gold-toothed waiter called Paco who thrilled Sandra Saxlingham with his diving at the sea-front swimming pool.

It was not until she was kissed in Bramfield's basement that at last she lost interest in legendary men and began to dream about a real one. For weeks after the encounter, she expected to see him again. She no longer forgot to clean her shoes. She washed her hair twice a week. She began to take care of her nails, and to think about clothes instead of books.

Sometimes, remembering the swarthiness of his skin, the un-English blackness of his hair, she felt sure the man in the basement had been a Spaniard. But Spaniards were rarely six-footers, and seldom did they have grey eyes. Of one thing only was she certain; he might or might not be Spanish, he could not be one of the waiters. There had been authority about him. It was impossible to imagine him in a starched white coat, a napkin draped over his forearm, bowing, being tipped. A *maître d'hotel*? A manager? No, that southern tan, the strong hands which had fended her off and then held her prisoner did not belong to a man who sat in an office all day, or supervised a public dining-room.

When September came, and then October, she was forced to accept that the man in the basement had been either a holidaymaker, or perhaps a day visitor merely.

By then she was learning shorthand and typing. She no longer left the house every morning with the exhilarating thought – Perhaps today I shall see him.

But she knew that some day, somewhere, they would meet again; and when they did, he would remember her, and fall in love with her.

On her twenty-first birthday, the day before she was due to cross the Channel, en route for her summer assignment in Andalusia, Grandplum gave Sophie the 1832 edition of Washington Irving's *The Alhambra*, and Aunt Rose gave her a swirling sea-green cloak, the hood encrusted with pearls and shimmering threads.

Sophie was enchanted by both gifts. She fastened the cloak and swept round the shabby drawing-room in the arrogant manner of a model. Then she laughed, and put back the hood, her long brown hair framing a face full of warmth and vitality. Boredom, petulance, the unsmiling hauteur of a mannequin were not among her natural expressions.

"Isn't it beautiful, Grandplum?" Her fingers touched the rich texture of the embroidery as lovingly as, a few minutes before, they had caressed the binding of his present. She gave Mrs. Steel a hug. "You're an angel to have made it for me when you have so much other work on hand."

"You know I like sewing for you, Sophie."

" 'Sewing', she calls it!" Sophie exclaimed. She knew that her aunt was an outstanding needlewoman who combined a superb technique with a flair for original design as outstanding as that of Rebecca Crompton in the 'thirties.

Sophie sank down on the windowseat, facing her grandfather who was seated in his Queen Anne winged chair. The folds of the cloak flowed round her tall, slender figure like the drapery on a Renaissance madonna.

"I shan't go to the Alhambra in the daytime when it's crowded with tourists. I shall go at night when it's moonlit and quiet, wearing this. A Spanish grandee will see me there, and beg me to share his castle in the sierras. But I'm afraid he'll change his mind when he sees me by daylight, in jeans," she added, laughing.

Smiling at her happy, excited mood, wondering if he would be alive to welcome her when she returned from Spain six months hence, old Mr. Lingwood watched the merriment fade from her face, to be replaced by the dreamy expression which had once been habitual but was now less characteristic of her.

Speaking of a castle in the sierras had reminded Sophie of someone she had never quite forgotten. The stranger who, four and a half years ago, had been the first man to kiss her.

For months he had filled her daydreams. Night after night she had switched off her bedside lamp, not because she was too sleepy to continue reading, but in order to lie in the darkness, making up a new episode in a romantic adventure which, in time and place, ranged from modern Antarctica to fifteenth-century Aragon. The only constant factor was that she was always the heroine of these dramas, and he was always the hero. She never gave him a name, partly because no English name seemed appropriate, and partly because she was so certain that one day she would know his real name. But sometimes, because he fitted perfectly into the part of a Spanish nobleman in the stirring

12

reign of Queen Isabella, she gave him a title – Lord of the Sierras.

In this role, he would carry her off to his stronghold in the high mountains, either to force her to marry him, or with even less honourable intentions. Innumerable times, in her mind, had Sophie enacted her capture, the wild night ride through the foothills, her attempted escape and, finally, the scene in his castle where, outwardly cool and defiant, she toyed with a midnight supper and dreaded the inevitable moment when the servants would withdraw and leave her alone with him. But usually, before this interesting juncture was reached, she had fallen asleep.

A year later, in the same way that the Lord of the Sierras had replaced her historical heroes, he in turn was usurped by a Frenchman.

Sophie met Guy on the Ile d'Oleron off the west coast of France. She was there to look after and speak English to the children of a Bordeaux hotelier who had a summer cottage on the island. Guy was a student, vacation-working in a nearby caravan camp. He made Sophie overcome her initial aversion to oysters, he taught her more French in two months than she had learned in two years at school and, when she was off duty and unencumbered by children, he kissed her.

He kissed her in secluded stretches of the lanes which connected the island's white-washed villages, and he kissed her while they were fossil-hunting on the rocky reefs which emerged from the sea at low tide. They kissed in the sea, and on the beach, and the only place she would not go with him was among the sandhills.

"But why not? It is more private there," said Guy, in the first of several arguments on the subject.

"That is why not, *mon ami*," replied Sophie, laughing.

She liked him, and she liked the feeling when he stroked her, and nibbled her ears, and murmured sweet things in French to her. But she was equally excited by her first taste of being abroad, and wary of anything which might jeopardise her freedom to travel more widely.

She had no special bent, no ambition for a career. She felt in her bones that her only talent was for marriage, and that all the best things in her life would begin when she fell in love seriously. But that might not happen for some time, and meanwhile it would be as well to see and do all the things which might not be possible afterwards.

Who knew what life held in store? The price of love for Aunt Rose had been a brief idyll, then widowhood. For her mother, marriage had brought an exciting journey out East, a baby and, soon after, death. Sophie might find herself marrying a man who required her to go to Bolivia with him. Or he might be the master of a tanker, at sea more often than at home. Or they might have to live somewhere miles from the nearest coast, like Birmingham, with no money to spare for seeing the world.

Therefore now was her chance to visit all the places which held magic for her. Mad Ludwig's castles in Bavaria. Lord Bothwell's grave near the ruins of Dragsholm in Denmark. The alpine meadows and glittering snowfields described by Arnold Lunn in one of her favourite books, *The Mountains of Youth*.

As time passed, it proved that Mr. Lingwood and his daughter had been wise not to worry about Sophie's failure to excel in examinations or to shine on the games field. In the wide world beyond the schoolroom, she had qualities which, for the footloose life she wished to lead, were more useful than a battery of A levels. She was sensible, reliable, and she had the gift of making friends everywhere. One job led to another, and wherever she travelled invariably there was a young man more than willing to help her to master his language.

After Guy there was Benedict, a Swiss boy, who taught her to ski, and clarified German grammar for her. After him there was curly-haired Paolo from whom she learned basic Italian. From Italy she went to Holland where, because so many Dutch people spoke English in addition to their own difficult-to-pronounce language, Sophie applied her mind to Spanish.

On the evening of her coming of age, which was also the eve of her departure, she went to the station to meet Kate Dilham, a friend whose home was in London, and who also had a summer job in Spain. The two girls were travelling together as far as the Costa Brava where Kate was to assist the English manager of a villa-letting agency. From there to the far south of Spain, Sophie would be on her own.

"You are lucky to have a car," said Kate, as they drove into the bowels of a Hovercraft at Dover the following morning. "If your job turns out to be ghastly, you can leave and look for something better. I shall be stuck for the whole season."

"My grandfather on my mother's side left me some money in trust for my twenty-first, and when I told Grandplum I wanted a car to go to Spain he advanced the cash before my birthday," Sophie explained.

The car was a small, secondhand station waggon, equipped with air beds and sleeping bags so that the girls could save money by camping rather than staying at hotels.

"If necessary I could have raised the money by selling my Kate Greenaway almanacs at Sotheby's," Sophie continued. "But I don't want to part with them unless I must."

Kate envied her friend's ability to supplement her earnings by buying and selling books, but even more she envied Sophie's emotional independence. Twice, Kate had believed herself to be in love, and both relationships had ended in disillusionment. A number of men had pursued Sophie, and she had seemed fond of them, but never to the extent of waiting anxiously for telephone calls and letters, and certainly never to the point of no return which Kate herself had passed, and which now she regretted.

Once, when they were discussing men in general, Kate had said, "What would you do if William threatened to stop seeing you if you wouldn't let him make love to you?"

"I should stop seeing *him*!" Sophie had answered, without hesitation. Then, because she guessed what had prompted the question, "I'm not in love with William, but even if I were I hope I wouldn't succumb to that antique gambit."

"You never seem to have any problems with your men friends," Kate had said moodily. "They look madly virile, but they all seem content to behave like Victorian curates."

Sophie had laughed. "Not always. More like Rasputin sometimes!"

"Really? Does William –?" Kate paused, half afraid the other girl might snub her curiosity. Sophie was an excellent confidante, but did not talk much about herself.

"I think sooner or later all men make the attempt," Sophie said thoughtfully. "What is off-putting is when one says firmly No, and they begin badgering."

"Most people seem to say Yes."

"Oh, codswallop, Kate! That's only what one hears on television and from trendy newspaper columnists. Anyway I would never be influenced by what *most* people do. I'm only interested in men who are interested in me as a whole person."

Remembering that conversation as the Hovercraft whirled them across the Channel in a cloud of spray, and with a roar of propellors which precluded all but shouted remarks, Kate wished she had been influenced by Sophie and not by the two men whose interest in her had proved to be both limited and short-lived.

"I wonder what Spanish men are like?" she remarked, when they had passed through the French Customs barrier at Calais.

The undertone of bitterness was not lost on Sophie. Poor old Kate, she thought compassionately. She's such a rotten judge of character. First a selfish sponger, and then some-one else's husband. Aloud, she said, "I've never known any – apart from hotel and restaurant staff. Kate, do you remember that waiter at the Imperial? Sandra Saxlingham's high-diving heart-throb?"

Kate nodded. "Sandra is getting married next month. I ran into her in Fenwick's coffee bar last week. She was shopping for her trousseau, and flashing a colossal great sapphire. Her fiancé must be loaded. He's a –."

But Sophie was no longer listening. For the second time in twenty-four hours she was thinking of the tall, black-haired man who perhaps, in a strange way, had helped to protect her from the pitfalls into which Kate had tumbled. True she had given up consciously day-dreaming about him, but the concept of an ideal man for whose coming it was worthwhile to wait had remained at the back of her mind, fixed there more securely than it would have been but for that traumatic encounter, years ago, in Bramfield's basement.

The fine weather held, and by the time they reached the Pyrenees and crossed the frontier into Spain, Kate had acquired a light tan. Sophie, who had been working in Switzerland before returning to Cliff Court for a week's breathing space between jobs, had been fairly tanned when they left England. Now she was as brown as most people at the end of a Spanish holiday. When she stopped for *gasolina* and the Spanish pump attendant brought her the change, he said something which brought a rosy tinge to her now deep golden skin.

"What did he say to you?" asked Kate, who could not remember ever seeing her friend blush so vividly.

"I think he's a southerner, not a Catalan, and that was an example of a *piropo*."

"Which is?"

"A flattering remark addressed to a girl in the street. Like a wolf whistle, but more specific. Years ago *piropos* were mainly poetic, but now they're generally rather coarse, I believe."

"Judging by your face, that one was pretty startling," commented Kate.

"He had such a thick regional accent I may have misunderstood him."

Before they separated, the girls were to spend one night in Barcelona at the home of Mr. and Mrs. Hellington, friends of Kate's uncle and aunt. The Hellingtons lived in an eight-storey block of expensive apartments in the centre of the city, and by the time she switched off the motor in the haven of the underground garage for residents' cars, Sophie was thankful to have finished driving for the day. Kate was an excellent navigator, but even so negotiating Barcelona's teeming traffic had been a tense experience.

Had they been free agents, staying in a cheap *pensión*, she would have spent the evening reading, with perhaps a short stroll to stretch her legs. But the Hellingtons were attending a party, and expected the girls to accompany them.

"It doesn't begin until nine, so there's plenty of time to have your hair done. Maria, my maid, will iron your dresses. You have brought some nice clothes for evening wear, I presume? Spanish women are extremely elegant, and always immaculately groomed," said Mrs. Hellington, looking with disapproval at the girls' car-creased pants and cotton tank tops.

Kate had short hair and was not unwilling to accept the appointment which Mrs. Hellington had made for her at a nearby salon. But Sophie had always disliked the ritual of a professional hair-do, and besides, she had washed her hair before they set out that morning, keeping it tucked inside a pale blue terry-turban until it was almost dry. All it needed now was to be thoroughly brushed. She thanked Mrs. Hellington for making the appointment, but added firmly that a catnap would do more for her looks.

"Oh, very well," said her hostess. "But you must certainly let Maria give you a manicure. Spanish girls of the upper class have their nails and hair done twice a week. Even girls from the poorer families take great care of their hands."

It was only as a concession to Mrs. Hellington, who was putting them up in considerable luxury if not the sort of lazy comfort they would have preferred, that Sophie decided to bind her long hair in a chignon. Grandplum and Aunt Rose did not care for it. William, the most worldly of her men friends, had preferred her with her hair up, and had given her an antique tortoiseshell comb, decorated with turquoise and seed pearls, to wear on top of her chignon.

When Mrs. Hellington saw the haute couture sea-green cloak, she was impressed. "A great improvement! One would hardly recognise you as the same girl, my dear," she said approvingly.

Under the cloak, Sophie was wearing a very plain long dress of uncrushable ivory material. Kate was in a dark red silk trouser suit. Mrs. Hellington was wearing green chiffon and an impressive display of diamonds and emeralds.

"You need a brooch on that suit, Kate. I'll lend you one." She hustled Kate off to her bedroom, leaving Sophie alone with Mr. Hellington.

"I expect you will find it takes some time to become accustomed to Spanish hours, lunch at two p.m., dinner at ten p.m. and so on," he remarked. "There is talk of doing away with the *siesta*, at least in the northern parts of Spain. In the south, in summer, it's impossible to work during the hottest hours of the day. I presume you're not adversely affected by intense heat, Miss Lingwood?"

"I hope not. I don't really know."

They made small talk until the others returned, Kate sparkling with borrowed ear-clips, a huge brooch, a heavy gold bracelet. She gave Sophie a glance expressive of helpless submission, and Sophie prepared to resist, with the utmost courtesy, Mrs. Hellington's attempts to bedizen her with borrowed glitter. However, the matter of the hair appointment seemed to have convinced their hostess that her second guest was not the compliant type.

The Hellingtons' car was an enormous glistening black limousine. Kate sat in the back, between them, and Sophie sat next to the chauffeur who was young and good-looking, and who, unseen by his employers, gave her the same bold, burning look she had received from the *gasolina* attendant. As they drove through the brightly lit city, she encountered similarly intense stares whenever she caught the eye of a man on the still-crowded pavements.

The party was taking place in an apartment even larger and more luxurious than the Hellingtons' flat. Sophie's cloak and Mrs. Hellington's furs were taken away by two of the several servants hovering attentively in the flower-banked, tapestry-hung entrance hall.

The owners of the apartment were an American couple who, according to Mrs. Hellington, were very rich, and very important and influential. Sophie disliked them from the moment when Mrs. Hackenbacker's limp fingers slithered out of her own firm handclasp, and Mrs. Hackenbacker's lips stretched in an artificial beam while her cold, pale eyes took note of her guest's lack of jewels.

"Heavens! There's enough loot in here to re-stock Cartier's," murmured Kate, as the girls followed the Hellingtons among the throng of chattering guests.

"Yes," agreed Sophie, unimpressed.

Clearly the Hellingtons and the Hackenbackers moved in circles where the possession and display of wealth was of first importance. It was a milieu to which she did not and had no wish to belong. Grandplum and Rose Steel had taught her to admire an antique amethyst more than a large modern diamond, wild lilac more than expensive roses with no scent, and people whose minds were rich even if they had no money.

The majority of the guests at the party were English or American, and those who were Spanish were speaking English. She had no opportunity to test her Spanish by listening to snatches of conversation. After an hour of laborious cocktail chit-chat, the noise and the cigarette smoke had begun to make her head ache, and once or twice she caught herself showing her boredom, and quickly had to pin on a smile which was as artificial as Mrs. Hackenbacker's.

She was sipping her third glass of champagne, longing for a cup of strong black coffee, and reflecting that people at a party resembled amoebae in the way that groups enlarged, split up and reformed, when through a gap in the heads she caught sight of a tall man. At the same moment, he looked at her.

Sophie gasped, and felt her heart lurch with shock and excitement. It was him . . . the Lord of the Sierras!

As they stared at each other, he began to smile with that very same quizzical glint she had never forgotten and to which, this time, she responded with a smile of unreserved

21

delight. Then the person beside her claimed her attention, and when she looked again he had disappeared.

I must have dreamed him, she thought. Perhaps I've had too much champagne on an empty stomach.

But she knew she had not imagined that lean, dark-skinned face and the oddly incongruous grey eyes. He was here in this room, and even though she could not see him, his presence made her tingle.

For the following ten minutes her emotion see-sawed between joy that at last, at this terrible party, the great adventure of her life had begun, and fear that he had not recognised her, or that, if he had, he was married and not free to follow up that involuntary gleam of interest. At last, when her spirits were beginning to sink with disappointment, a hand touched her shoulder, and she turned and there he was, beside her.

"Good evening," he said. "This is an unforeseen pleasure. I needn't ask how you are. You look wonderful – the only girl here who doesn't have to decorate herself like a Christmas tree to make an impression."

Sophie laughed, her hazel eyes shining. Relief and pleasure were effervescing inside her like the bubbles in her glass of champagne. He was waiting to shake hands, and as she transferred the glass to her left hand, she caught the swift glance with which he noticed the absence of rings.

"Surely you can't be enjoying this hubbub? Come and have dinner with me. I know a restaurant by the harbour where the food is good, and one can hear oneself speak."

"It's a tempting suggestion, but I'm here with Mr. and Mrs. Hellington, and I can't very well –"

"I shouldn't think they would mind – not if I explained the special circumstances." The grey eyes were brilliant with devilment. "Introduce me to Mrs. Hellington, and I'll put my case to her." He paused before he added blandly,

"If you've forgotten my name, it's Carlos Walsingham."

It was on the tip of her tongue to answer, "And I'm Sophie Lingwood – just in case *you* had forgotten." But she changed her mind. It would be interesting to see how he coped with that difficulty unaided.

As it happened, Mrs. Hellington was nearby. She was listening to a small, stout Spanish matron, but not with her full attention. Her eyes flickered hither and thither, appraising the people round about. She saw Sophie coming, and her pencilled eyebrows lifted slightly at the sight of Sophie's tall companion.

"Mrs. Hellington, may I introduce Carlos Walsingham?"

"How do you do?"

Jewelled fingers with crimson nails were extended to Carlos, who bowed and raised them to his lips, without actually kissing them. Then, with Sophie, he was presented to Señora Ruiz.

"I am hoping you will allow me to filch Miss Lingwood from you for the rest of the evening," he said (Sophie suppressed a smile at his easy use of her surname which, seconds ago, he had not known.) "Tomorrow I am leaving Barcelona, so tonight is our only opportunity to renew an old acquaintance."

"Why yes, certainly . . . by all means. I'll see you at breakfast, my dear. Don't keep her out too late, Mr. Walsingham. She has a long journey tomorrow." With a smile, Mrs Hellington dismissed them.

In the hall, Sophie said, "I have a cloak somewhere . . ."

Carlos spoke in Spanish to a manservant who bowed and disappeared. While they were waiting, he said mockingly, "Let me see, where *was* it we met last? Davos? St. Tropez? Brussels?"

"It's so long ago, I'm surprised you remember it at all."

"How could I forget those golden eyes? Ah, here is your

23

wrap." He took it from the servant, unfurled it, and placed it round her shoulders.

In the ground floor lobby he gave his key-ring to a porter, explaining, "We shall have to wait a few minutes while he fetches my car from wherever he has managed to park it. So you also are a bird of passage? Where are you going tomorrow? Back to England?"

"No, south . . . to Andalusia."

"Really? So am I. Perhaps we shall meet again there."

"Perhaps," she agreed, smiling.

With any other man, she would have been cautious, keeping up some reserve until she knew more about him. But had he been any other man she would not have made it so easy for him to extract her from the party.

An expensive white car with the hood down glided up to the entrance, driven by the uniformed porter. Carlos thanked and tipped him. He put Sophie into the passenger seat, taking care that the folds of her cloak were not caught in the door when he closed it. Then he walked round the long, streamlined bonnet to take his place behind the wheel.

"A French car, a Spanish first name, and an English surname. You are truly cosmopolitan," she said presently, as with the ease of familiarity he drove through the city, never finding himself in the wrong lane of traffic as she had done several hours earlier.

His hands on the wheel were gypsy-dark against the white cuffs of his dress shirt. He was a relaxed, uncompetitive driver, she noted approvingly. Not for him the skidding arrival at traffic lights, the fast showy getaway. In Sophie's observation, men who did drive in that fashion were either immature or insecure. Carlos Walsingham was not a green boy in the first flush of manhood, nor did he need a powerful car to make women warm to him and men respect him. He had not the smooth Latin handsomeness of the Hellingtons' *chófer* and the other young Spaniards she had seen here. Yet, even if he wore the dusty denims and bright orange helmet of one of the building site labourers, there would be something about him to make most women look twice.

"My mother was Spanish," he explained. "As a young girl she was sent to England to be spared the violence and danger of the *Movimiento* – the Civil War. She married an Englishman who was killed in action towards the end of the World War. When I went to school, she returned to Spain and married again. From that time my life was divided between an English boarding school and the house of my Spanish stepfather. Two more dissimilar backgrounds it is difficult to imagine," he added dryly. "And you, Miss Lingwood? What combination of genes has produced such admirable results?"

"As far as I know, my genes are all English," she answered. "But I was born in the Far East, and lately I've travelled a good deal, although this is my first visit to Spain."

"Let us hope it will be a memorable one."

Tonight will be unforgettable, thought Sophie, studying his strong-boned profile and well-shaped head.

They were driving along part of the city's extensive waterfront. "Those are the night ferries to the Balearics," said Carlos, indicating the steamers moored at adjoining, brightly lit wharves. "The big modern one is bound for Mallorca, and the other for Menorca. They'll reach the islands at sunrise tomorrow. And that is a reconstruction of the *Santa Maria*," he added, as they approached the mooring of a fifteenth-century galleon.

"The ship in which Christopher Columbus made his first voyage to the New World?"

"Correct; but in Spain he is Cristóbal Colon. I was often in trouble at school because I forgot that history is not the same in every country."

The *restaurante* to which he took her was not the kind of establishment frequented by Hellingtons and Hackenbackers. It was comfortable and very clean, but it lacked a spectacular decor, enormous menus, and the frequent tableside *flambé*ing which Sophie had learnt, in France, to regard as a gimmicky waste of brandy.

As they walked down the long narrow room where all but one of the tables were occupied by family parties from the prosperous artisan class, she was surprised to hear Carlos saying good evening, in Spanish, to the other patrons, and being greeted by them. She was conscious of the women's black eyes appraising her, but theirs was not a cold curiosity, and their murmured comments were flattering.

"*Guapa* is a word *you* will hear very often in Spain," he said, when they were seated. "It has many shades of meaning from 'pretty' to 'beautiful'. As you heard it just now it meant 'very beautiful.'"

Sophie was about to reply that a reasonable command of the Spanish language had been an essential qualification for her summer job, but the waiter was approaching. She left the remark unspoken, and merely smiled her acknowledgment of the compliment. He was entirely Spanish when he was paying compliments, she thought.

"If this is your first time in Spain, we must have *paella*," said Carlos. "In the tourist places, often it is not as it should be. But here, where local people eat, the *paella* is excellent. You're hungry, I hope?"

"Very hungry," she confirmed. "Do you come here often? You seem to know everyone."

"No, I don't know them. In Spain it's the custom to say hello to one's fellow diners. The Spanish are a very friendly people."

"So I've noticed. Even the half-Spanish are exceptionally affable."

He grinned. "I don't think you would have difficulty in making friends in any country, Miss Lingwood. Perhaps with your own sex sometimes, but never with mine."

The waiter brought sherry, and a tray of *tapas* including morsels of squid fried in crisp golden batter, stuffed dates, plump black olives, salty pickled anchovies, and slices of marbled red *chorizo*, a delicious garlicky sausage oozing a bright orange juice and calling for sound teeth and a robust digestion, both of which Sophie possessed.

"I have a confession to make. I cannot recall your first name," Carlos said suddenly.

"Sophie."

"Short for Sophonisba? Sophronia?"

"No, thank goodness! Just Sophie. Are there really such names, or did you make them up?"

"By no means. Sophronia is one of the girls in a book by Boccaccio, and Sophonisba was Hannibal's niece. She sounds a rather formidable female. Sophie has an eighteenth century flavour. One thinks of those charming creatures painted by Franz-Christoph Janneck."

It so happened that Sophie was acquainted with some paintings by Janneck. The charming creatures she remembered had all been displaying a startling expanse of bosom below faces with the sort of vacuous prettiness she associated with Bunny Girls and Penthouse Pets.

For a moment, at the back of her mind, there flicked the uncomfortable thought that perhaps Carlos's taste in women was for pretty, sexy, rather silly girls without a thought in their heads beyond pleasing the man of the moment; and, even more discomfiting, that he might have mistaken her for one of them.

But then the *paella* arrived, a feast of glistening yellow rice steaming in a wide shallow pan, and decked with purple-shelled mussels, pink prawns, shreds of scarlet pepper, green peas and succulent chicken joints. With it came wine, and a basket of fresh crusty bread baked in an old-fashioned oven and as different from factory-steamed loaves as canned stew from home-made hot-pot.

As the waiter piled their plates high, and poured out the wine, Sophie dismissed the tiny doubt, tucked a corner of a large gingham napkin inside the neckline of her evening dress, and prepared to attack her supper with the same uninhibited enthusiasm displayed by the stout Spanish wife at the next table.

It was midnight when they left the restaurant. "Now where shall I take you to dance?" Carlos pondered, as they strolled to the car.

"Are you mad? After that huge meal, I can scarcely walk!" said Sophie, laughing.

"Then we'll drive instead." He indicated the hills surrounding the city. "I'll take you up there to see the view."

She shook her head. "I must go back now, Carlos. I haven't a latch-key, and it won't be the Hellingtons who wait up for me. It will be Maria, their maid, who looked terribly tired this afternoon."

Rather to her surprise, he did not argue. Driving her back to the apartment, he said, "How are you travelling tomorrow? By air, I presume?"

"No, by road."

"You have your own car?"

"Yes."

"Where will you stay tomorrow night? With other friends along the coast road?"

"The Hellingtons aren't friends of mine. They have a business connection with relations of Kate Dilham, the girl

28

who has been travelling with me. Tomorrow she goes to Llafranch, and I shall potter on south. I haven't a rigid programme. I'll drive till I'm tired, and then stop."

He dropped the subject and began to talk about Switzerland. In the restaurant, most of their conversation had been about the other countries of Europe, and the places they knew and liked or disliked.

A night porter was on duty in the lobby of the block of flats. The lift was at ground level.

Sophie half expected Carlos to shake hands, and walk out of her life as abruptly as he had re-entered it. But he said, "I'll see you to your door."

As the lift passed the first floor landing, he turned her towards him, and put back the hood of her cloak. Then he took her in his arms and kissed her.

When the lift reached the fourth floor and stopped, Carlos let her go. They walked to the Hellingtons' door, and he pressed the gilt bell push. When the door was opened by Maria, he said, "*Buenas noches, querida*," and disappeared down the staircase.

Listening to the sound of his footsteps receding down the green marble stairs, she realised belatedly that she had not thanked him, or even answered his goodnight.

"Sophie! At last! Where have you been? Who is this fabulous man I've been hearing about? Why didn't you tell me you had a Spanish millionaire up your sleeve?"

As Sophie entered the lamplit room where Kate was reading in bed, her friend flung aside the magazine and began to fire excited questions at her.

"Spanish millionaire? What *are* you talking about, Kate?" Sophie exclaimed bewilderedly. She was still in a daze from those heart-stopping moments in Carlos's arms when past and present had fused, and left her as deeply, if differently, shaken by his second embrace as she had been by his first.

"Well, that's what Mrs. Hackenbacker told Mrs. Hellington. According to her, he's the most eligible bachelor between the Pyrenees and Gibraltar, and no end of husband-hunting *señoritas* and matchmaking *señoras* are going to be livid when they hear he has been snaffled an English girl."

"Oh, Kate, what absolute nonsense!" Sophie sank on to the other twin bed, and kicked off her gold kid sandals. "Mrs. Hackenbacker has her facts wrong. To begin with, he isn't Spanish."

"No, she didn't say he was, actually," agreed Kate. "She said his father was a member of a very rich English merchant banking family, and his mother inherited a wine fortune. Not surprisingly your Carlos has a flair for making money on his own account. He owns hotels and motels and villas all over the place."

"He isn't 'my Carlos'," said Sophie. "I met him once, ages ago, and tonight at the party we were both very bored and very hungry, so he took me to have a *paella*. But we're both leaving town in the morning, and heaven knows when, if ever, I shall see him again."

"But he did kiss you goodnight in the lift?"

"H-how did you know?"

"It was a guess. You don't usually float about with that bedazzled expression on your face. Where did you meet him the first time?"

"In ... Switzerland," Sophie said untruthfully. It made her uncomfortable to lie, but the truth was too private and, to someone like Kate, too unbelievable.

"He must have made a big impression on you if you let him kiss you tonight. With your puritan outlook on life, a goodnight kiss on the second date is pretty significant," Kate

30

said, rather sarcastically.

"I'm not a puritan, Kate. I've kissed a lot of people. I just don't intend to sleep with anyone until I'm certain I love them, by which time I'll know if they love me," Sophie said mildly.

Her friend flushed, and pleated the sheet. "I'm sorry, love. That was foul of me. I suppose the truth is I'm jealous because I've had two lousy affairs, whereas you've kept on the straight and narrow, and your virtue is about to be rewarded."

"A *paella* is not a proposal, Kate," Sophie said, smiling, and starting to undress. "What else did you hear about him?"

"Mrs. Hackenbacker, who is definitely not one of my favourite people, said most southern Spaniards had Moorish blood in their veins, and from what she had heard Carlos Walsingham had Moorish habits as well."

"Silly woman! As the Arab occupation of Spain lasted for nearly eight centuries, naturally the Andalusians are more Moorish than anything else. What did she mean by Moorish habits? I don't think he smokes, but he's definitely not a non-drinker."

"That's what Mrs. Hellington asked, and Mrs. Hackenbacker sniggered and said that probably it wasn't possible to keep a proper harem nowadays, but everyone said that Carlos had more than one love-nest." Kate paused. "I'm not telling you this to be nasty, Sophie. But if you really do like him, it's as well to know the gossip about him."

Sophie went to the bathroom to take off her make-up. She left the door open, and asked, "What did Mr. Hackenbacker say? Or didn't the husbands contribute to the discussion?"

"They looked rather sheepish, I thought, as if they might both have a popsie tucked away somewhere. The more I see

31

of the two Mrs. Hs, the less I blame them if they have. The only thing Mr. Hackenbacker said was that young Walsingham had a vurry, vurry shrewd business brain. How old is Carlos? Do you know?"

"Thirty, perhaps. I'm not sure. Excuse me for a few minutes, will you?" Sophie closed the bathroom door.

When she emerged, some time later, she was relieved to find that Kate had fallen asleep. She let down her chignon, brushed her hair, and put the antique comb safely in its padded box. Then she switched off both bedside lamps, drew back the ivory silk curtains, and climbed into bed. But although she was physically tired, she had far too much on her mind to be able to sleep.

As Mrs. Hellington had informed the girls that she always had breakfast in bed, clearly it was curiosity about Sophie's relationship with Carlos Walsingham which prompted her to join them at the breakfast table the next morning.

"Did you have a good time, my dear? Where did Mr. Walsingham take you for dinner?"

"I don't know the name of the restaurant. It was a small place somewhere along the waterfront. He said they did a particularly good *paella* there."

At this moment Maria appeared carrying a basket holding about ten dozen carnations. It was not a presentation basket from a florist's shop, with the blooms already arranged in a stiff display. This was a large serviceable basket such as Sophie had seen in flower markets all over Europe. On one side of the handle the carnations were dark red, on the other they were white. They filled the room with their scent.

"For you, *señorita*," announced Maria.

"For me?" Sophie echoed, taken aback.

The maid nodded, and handed her an envelope on which

Sophie's name and the Hellingtons' address were written in a strong, clearly legible hand.

"Heavens! That lot would cost a fortune in London," remarked Kate.

"Carnations are not cheap here at present," said Mrs. Hellington. "Mr. Walsingham must be very taken with you, Sophie."

Sophie had slit the envelope and extracted the single sheet of paper. Unfolding it, she read *There is a poem by the Marqués de Santillana which begins –*" The rest of the note was in Spanish. There was no signature.

"What does he say?" asked Kate eagerly. "Does he want to see you again today?"

"If you would like to stay on for a few days, we shall be delighted to put you up, my dear," added Mrs. Hellington.

Slowly, Sophie looked up from the words on the paper. "It's kind of you, but I must leave Barcelona this morning. I've promised to start work next week, and I must allow time for possible breakdowns and for seeing one or two places on the way. This is just a polite note to thank me for dining with him last night."

"I know I'm being nosey, but was it really only a polite note?" asked Kate later, when she and Sophie were re-packing their overnight bags. "I can't believe that even very rich men make extravagant gestures with carnations to girls they expect never to see again."

"There's a possibility that we might meet somewhere in the south," answered Sophie. "But it isn't likely. He doesn't know where I'm going, or why; and, if he's in the hotel business, I should imagine his centre of operations is at Málaga or Marbella. They're both a long way from my patch of the Costa del Sol. Kate, what *am* I to do with so many carnations? They'll die if I take them with me."

"My dear Sophie, these are the sort of problems you'll

have to face if you're going to make a habit of enslaving millionaires," replied Kate, with a grin.

It was soon after nine o'clock when Sophie drove up the ramp from the underground garage, and waved a last goodbye to Kate who was spending the day looking round Barcelona before catching a late afternoon bus to Llafranch, a resort to the north.

The hall porter had given Sophie directions for leaving the city, and as soon as she was on the outskirts where it was easy to park for a few minutes, she stopped the car to read again the note from Carlos.

An extract from a fifteenth-century poem was not as easy to translate as modern prose, but as far as she could make out the lines meant – *A girl from Bores, down by La Lama, made me in love. I thought that love had forgotten me, as one who had long ceased to have those pains that burn lovers worse than a flame. But I saw that beauty, so lovely to look at, with a pleasing face, fresh as a rose, with such colouring as I have never seen in another woman.*

Before she left Barcelona behind her, she stopped the car a second time. She noticed two women sitting on chairs on the pavement on the shady side of the street. One was very old, dressed in black. The other was young and soon to have a child. On impulse, Sophie pulled in to the kerb. Filling her arms with all but a few carnations, she crossed the road.

Smiling she said in her unpracticed Castilian, "*Senoras*, a young man has given me these lovely flowers, but I have a long way to travel, and in the heat of my car they will die before I arrive at my destination. May I give them to you for your pleasure?"

Their startled exclamations followed her as she returned to the car. As she slid behind the wheel and waved, the younger woman shouted, "*Buen viaje, señorita!*"

It was almost noon before Sophie stopped for the third time. She had come to a stretch of road where the Mediterranean was only yards from the dusty verges of the highway. Although she had not seen anyone bathing, the calm blue sea, glittering in the brilliant sunlight, was an irresistible temptation to her.

The rear part of the car being equipped with curtains for when the girls spent the night in it, she had no problem about where to change into her bathing suit. Within five minutes of pulling off the road, she was running across the hot sand to the water's edge.

Probably by Spanish standards the sea was still too cold for enjoyable swimming. To Sophie, accustomed from childhood to braving the tumbling grey-green shallows of the English Channel, the water temperature here was merely refreshing.

Mocuela de Bores, allá do La Lama, pusome enamores. A girl from Bora, down by La Lama, made me in love.

As she swam, and floated, and swam again, the opening line of the poem echoed in her mind, and with it the memory of last night's kiss in the lift. So far, everything he had said and done, everything about him, had confirmed the myth she had built round him since their first brief meeting, years ago. Now the only flaw in her happiness was not knowing when they would meet again.

As she waded out of the water, her long hair streaming down her back, Sophie was conscious of hunger. Less than a quarter of a mile further on she could see a white building painted with the red letters BAR. Perhaps it was also a café where, when her hair was dry, she could buy a light lunch and an iced drink.

As she turned to stroll back to the car, her heart began suddenly to race, but not from the exertion of her swim, or the heat which made the hills shimmer. Beside her car was another, a sleek white French car. And where, fifteen minutes ago, the beach had been a deserted stretch of sand and rock outcrop, there was now a circle of shadow cast by a gaily-coloured sunbrella. In the shade, on one of two long beach chairs, lounged a tall, dark-skinned man.

Sophie began to run. "Carlos! What are you doing here? she demanded, when she reached the sunbrella. She made no attempt to hide her pleasure at seeing him.

He had risen to his feet at her approach, and was holding out the pale blue terry robe she had dropped on the sand with her clogs and sun-glasses.

"Thank you." She slid her arms into the sleeves, and fastened the sash.

Today, Carlos was wearing a pair of pale Dacron pants, and a short-sleeved cotton-knit shirt which showed that the strong, straight shoulders she had noticed with approval last night owed nothing to the skill of whoever had tailored his dinner jacket. He might be rich, but if he indulged in rich living it did not show at his jawline or waistline.

"Weren't you expecting me?" he asked.

"No, of course not. Why should I? How did you know where to find me? Or is this a coincidence?"

"By no means. I bribed your hall porter to telephone me as soon as you left the building. From Sitges to here I've been following you. It isn't difficult to tail a car with GB plates."

Sophie said nothing. She moved a short distance away to wring out her hair. Then she slipped on a stretchy bandeau which she kept in the pocket of the robe, and also her large dark glasses. No one had ever laid siege to her in this dashing fashion before, and she was rather overwhelmed by it.

"You forgot to shake hands with me," said Carlos. "In Spain one must always shake hands. Even the teenagers do it when groups of them meet in the street, or on the beach."

She put her hand into his, and felt a tremor run up to her shoulder as the well-shaped dark hand closed over her smaller, lighter-brown one. He gripped it for an instant, then he kissed it.

"I thought only married women had their hands kissed?" she said, catching her breath.

"Yes," he agreed. "But you are English, and I am half English, so we may adapt the custom to suit ourselves. You're thirsty, I expect. Let me give you a drink."

He had brought with him a large insulated food bag, and also a smaller hamper fitted with all the cutlery, plates and drinking vessels needed for a picnic *a deux*. To her amazement, she saw that everything was made of hand-beaten, crested silver.

Carlos noticed her astonishment. "It was given to me by one of my Spanish great-uncles. At the time these things were made they were probably not much more expensive than fine china. They're unbreakable, like plastic, but considerably more attractive, don't you think?"

"Indeed I do! Thank you" – this as he handed her one of the silver goblets filled with some ice-cold golden liquid from a vacuum jug.

"It's only fruit juice. I don't take wine when I'm driving on fast roads, and I didn't think you would mind a soft drink with your lunch. Apart from the safety aspect, wine at midday makes people drowsy. A *siesta* can be very pleasant" – with a glint in his grey eyes which made her look away towards the sea – "but in general I prefer to stay awake, and drink wine in the evening."

"I was planning to have egg and chips at the next café along the road," said Sophie presently, unfolding a fine linen napkin and watching him serve the salad.

"There's a Spanish poem which says life is always unexpected. *Cuando pitos, flautas; cuando flautas, pitos.*

When you expect flutes, you get whistles. And when you expect –"

"Fried eggs, you find yourself eating prawns in aspic from a silver dish," she finished for him. "That reminds me, I haven't yet thanked you for the heavenly carnations ... and for the other poem."

"Did you find someone to translate it for you?"

"No –" She was about to add 'it wasn't necessary' but changed it to – "Now you can tell me what it means."

"With pleasure. On one condition."

"Which is?"

"That tonight you have dinner with me again."

"It's hardly possible, is it? If you drive at your car's normal cruising speed, you'll be miles ahead of me by this evening."

"True, but I happen to have an appointment in Valencia which will last at least an hour, possibly longer. There's a good hotel a few kilometres before one enters Alicante. In the high season a reservation is essential, but they won't be fully booked at this time of year. At the speed you've been driving this morning, you'll arrive there with plenty of time to rest before I meet you for dinner, and take you to see something of Alicante."

Sophie hesitated. Ought she to demur? Ought she to keep him guessing a little?

Always it had seemed to her that when a girl liked a man very much, it was stupid and pointless to dissemble. *Mocuela de Bores ... pusome en amores.* Carlos was making no bones about his liking for her. Why pretend not to reciprocate?

"In that case I'd be delighted to have dinner with you," she told him. "Mrs. Hellington says you are in the hotel business yourself. Are you recommending me to stay at one of your own establishments?"

38

He laughed, and shook his head. "I have no property on this coast, only in the south. But the present manager of the Miramar used to work for me, so I can promise you every attention to your comfort."

"Another example of whistles and flutes," said Sophie. "I was planning to try a Spanish camp site. That's how Kate and I travelled through France."

"Camping is excellent for students, and for families who want a holiday which is cheap but more adventurous than a package trip," said Carlos, with a shrug. "But even the well-run camps are generally too noisy and crowded for comfort. The best place to stay in Spain is at a Government-owned *parador*. They are equal to the finest hotels, but extremely moderate in their charges. Some of them are in buildings which once were royal palaces."

Even without the soporific effect of wine, the delicious lunch, the comfort of the canvas reclining chair, the sea air and the increasing heat combined to make Sophie very much inclined to doze as she sipped her second cup of coffee.

Carlos showed no sign of drowsiness although, as a concession to the brilliance of the light, he had put on a pair of tinted glasses. By partially concealing his English eyes, they accentuated his Spanish heredity, and the Moorish strain, still strong after twenty generations.

He said, "You have charming feet, Sophie. Most women's toes are deformed from wearing tight shoes. Aren't you hot now in that beach robe? If you take it off, your bikini will be dry by the time we leave here."

"Yes, you're right." She sat up and shed the blue robe. Then she wished she had not. Her bikini, chosen for energetic swimming as well as basking, was not a particularly skimpy one, nor was she normally self-conscious. But Carlos, unlike many men, was not sly in his appraisial of her figure. His interest in her slim golden body was as open as his study of her feet, and it made her shy enough to say hurriedly, "I think I'll have another swim. How about you?"

"It's much too soon after lunch. We can walk, if you like." He sprang up and held out his hand to her.

The shuttle of cars on the highway had virtually ceased, for now it was nearly two o'clock and the Spanish lunch break had begun. Without the intrusive drone of passing vehicles, and with no tall hotels or new apartment blocks in sight – for this stretch of the coast was as yet undeveloped – the beach had become as peaceful and private as the whole eastern seaboard must have been before millions of sun-seeking northerners began to pour over the frontier.

Strolling across the hot sand, Sophie remembered the winter afternoons when, muffled against the cold wind and the spray from the wild Channel breakers, she had trudged along the shore below Cliff Court, dreaming and wondering about this man. Now here she was, hand in hand with him, and tonight he was going to show her the sights of Alicante and tell her the meaning of the poem.

"You must get yourself a shady hat," said Carlos. "The Spanish sun can give headaches to people who aren't accustomed to it."

"Yes, and it will make my hair dull if I'm not careful," she said, pulling off the bandeau and shaking out her smoky-brown mane.

He stopped walking, and drew her into his arms. "That would be a pity. At present your hair is like silk."

She thought he was going to kiss her again, but after holding her close for some moments, he let her go and said briskly, "We had better resume our journeys."

Sophie was still in her swimsuit when the white car sped away south, and was soon lost to sight in the heat haze blurring the highway. The interior of her car was like an oven as she put on the clothes she had worn earlier. But once the car was moving, with all the windows wide open, it was not unbearably hot.

For most of the afternoon she was travelling past acres of orange groves. The scent of the blossom blew through the car and mingled with the scent of the carnations. At the side of the road where the province of Valencia marched with the province of Alicante, there was a sign – *La casa de la primavera.*

"The home of spring," murmured Sophie, enchanted.

She arrived at the hotel which Carlos had recommended with two hours to spare before their rendezvous. The foyer overlooked the hotel car-park, and the girl on duty at the reception desk must have spotted the foreign registration on the dusty little estate car. As Sophie approached her, she smiled and said, "Good afternoon."

The bedroom to which Sophie was shown overlooked the palm-shaded hotel gardens and, beyond it, the Mediterranean. She washed her hair under the shower, then sat, wrapped in a bath towel, lazily fanning her hair with her portable dryer, and thinking about Carlos Walsingham.

Some time later, feeling far too excited and restless to pass the time by reading, she went down to the lobby to buy some Spanish stamps. She was standing beside a revolving display rack, choosing coloured postcards, when Carlos entered the lobby. He was carrying a suitcase, and it was only then that she realised he also was putting up at the Miramar. Somehow she had formed the impression that he would be spending the night at a hotel in Alicante.

"Hello again," he said, smiling at her. "I finished my business earlier than I anticipated."

While he was registering, a Spaniard came out of an office adjoining the lobby. The two men greeted each other

41

cordially, and Carlos introduced the Spaniard to Sophie. He was the manager, and he spoke English. After exchanging one or two conventional remarks with him, Sophie moved away to pay the receptionist for the postcards. While she was doing so, Carlos enquired, in Spanish, about the manager's wife and children.

Presently, only half listening, she heard the Spaniard remark, "But you, Carlos, you are still determined to keep your freedom, eh? How long have you had this pretty creature in tow? And how much longer will she enjoy your generosity? Not more than a few weeks, I suppose?"

"You exaggerate, Jorge. I am not an inveterate womaniser. But if a girl is looking for an adventure, and throws herself at me, what do you expect me to do? I am not such a roué as you make out, my friend, but neither am I a monk and, as you say, she is charming. You've given us adjoining rooms, of course?"

"Of course – and no doubt it will not be long before the connecting door is unlocked and you are *en suite,* lucky devil!"

"No comment."

Carlos came over to Sophie, and put his hand on her shoulder. In English, he said, "Give me fifteen minutes to have a shower, and then I will join you for a drink on the terrace, and we will consider how to spend the evening."

Apparently her face showed nothing of her feelings. Without waiting for her assent, he gave her a pat and disappeared into the lift.

CHAPTER TWO

SOPHIE spent the night in a grove of tall palm trees on the outskirts of an inland town called Elche. She had intended to find a hotel, until she noticed the wigwam sign which indicated a nearby camping ground. It was easier to follow the arrow than to venture into the town centre.

Because it was so early in the year, there was plenty of room in the camp even for a late arrival. She parked the car as far as possible from the other campers. On the way to the wash-room to clean her teeth, she threw the remaining carnations into a rubbish bin, and left the basket alongside where anyone who had a use for it was welcome to take it. Back at the car, she drew the curtains, undressed, and slid inside her sleeping bag. Then she buried her face in the pillow, and wept for the foolish but lovely illusion which Carlos had shattered into irreparable fragments.

"There's nothing to beat 'Early to bed, early to rise', is there?" said a cheery Midlander in a singlet and long khaki shorts, passing Sophie on her way to the wash-room at six o'clock the next morning.

When she saw her reflection in the mirror above the handbasin, a grim little smile twisted her lips. A less shining morning face it was hard to imagine.

Last night she had been too upset and exhausted to bother about taking off her make-up. Now her eyelids were not only swollen from the long bout of stifled weeping, but ringed by dark panda-like circles of smeared mascara.

She looked better after a wash, and she felt better after two aspirins and a cup of black coffee made with water boiled on her portable gas ring. But she knew it would be a long time before she recovered from the shock and pain and humiliation of yesterday.

Being essentially a transit camp, rather than a destination, by ten o'clock the El Palmeral camp was deserted but for one caravan, a large blue frame tent, and Sophie's car.

She spent part of the morning lying in the sun by the camp swimming pool. Then a Frenchwoman sat down near her, and asked if she had been to see the Huerta del Cura across the road. To avoid the conversation which clearly the question was intended to initiate, Sophie replied that she had not visited the Priest's Garden, but would do so at once.

Until she entered the garden, it had been in her mind to spend the day pulling herself together and, tomorrow, to cancel her summer engagement by telegram, retrace her route to the frontier, and find some other employment in part of Europe where there was very little likelihood of running into Carlos Walsingham.

But as she wandered in the Huerta del Cura, planted with a thousand palms as well as lemon, almond, orange and pomegranate trees, she began to realise that she could not let down Piet Veenveld and, even if she had no obligation to him, it would be silly to miss all that Spain had to offer merely because a half-Spanish philanderer had made a fool of her.

No, that isn't true, she thought, gazing across a lily pool at the mysterious face of a copy of the Lady of Elche, an ancient stone bust unearthed in 1897 and now a national treasure in the Prado Museum at Madrid.

I made a fool of myself. I had the crazy vanity to suppose that a man like Carlos – very rich as well as very attractive – could fall in love with me on sight. It was true what he told his friend Jorge. From his point of view, I *did* appear to throw myself at him. How was he to know that, to me, he wasn't a stranger?

In another part of the garden there was an imperial palm tree which, according to the leaflet she had been given at the grate, was a unique botanical specimen. In 1880, when the tree was already very old, it had suddenly changed its sex and borne seven sprigs. Now, at the age of one hundred and fifty years, without probably another century to live, it consisted of eight towering palms growing from a single immense trunk.

As Sophie stared at this strange tree with outwardly rapt interest, inwardly she was carrying on an argument. She was willing to admit that most of the blame for yesterday's débâcle lay with her; but was Carlos blameless? From what she had heard, a born-and-bred Spaniard could be forgiven for supposing that a girl travelling on her own abroad, a girl who went out to dinner with a man she didn't know, was not of the highest moral character. But Carlos, the son of an Englishman, educated in England, had no excuse for mistaking an adventurous girl for an adventuress. Furthermore, if he was as experienced as people made out, it was high time he learnt to distinguish between a girl who was ready to give her heart to him, and one who was willing merely to go to bed with him.

If she had been stupidly naïve, by far his most culpable action had been to send her a love poem.

A girl from Bores ... made me in love. I thought that love had forgotten me ...

What girl, either Spanish or English, who read those lines would not think, and be justified in thinking, that the man who sent them had in mind something far more serious than a casual affair?

In the afternoon, she slept in the back of the car. When she woke, some new campers had arrived. After a shower, he went for a stroll along the street outside the camp gates. Not far away another gateway in a high wall surrounding a commercial palm grove. Sophie bought a kilo of dates in the shop close to the entrance. The shopkeeper told her that Elche had the only fruiting palm forests in Europe. Tasting a date made her realise it was nearly thirty hours since her last meal.

Fortunately the camp had a small restaurant. After supper, as only half the tables were occupied, she ordered a glass of Spanish brandy to drink with her coffee, and began to read the book about the Alhambra which Grandplum had given her for her birthday.

In the spring of 1829, the Author of this Work, whom curiosity had brought into Spain, made a rambling expedition from Seville to Granada in company with a friend.

By the time she had turned the first page of the Introduction, Sophie had escaped from the real world into Washington Irving's world of one hundred and fifty years ago. For a little while she was able to forget her bruised emotions.

By seven o'clock the next morning, she was on the last lap of her journey, determined to expunge from her mind all that had happened between the time of her arrival, with Kate, in Barcelona, and her abrupt departure, the night before last, from the Hotel Miramar.

This was easier said than done, as she discovered when she was driving through the strange and sinister desert country between Vera and Almería. She was hoping that she would not have the bad luck to break down in this arid, shadeless region of eroded canyons and scorched escarpments, when a glance in her driving mirror made her throat constrict with alarm. Coming up fast behind her was a long low white car.

When it swung out, swept past, and was gone in a swirl

of white dust, she began to tremble with relief. She had not glimpsed the driver, but the car had had a Swiss registration.

At Almería the road rejoined the coast, and she was glad to see the Mediterranean again, and to know that by teatime she would have arrived. The mileometer had clocked over two thousand miles since she had checked the mileage in the driveway at Cliff Court, and she was beginning to feel that she had been driving for weeks rather than days.

At Aguadulce, the small resort where she stopped for her lunch break, she had another momentary fright. She was sitting in the car in the shade of a block of apartments, and finishing up the dates she had bought at Elche, when a man came out of the building and looked in her direction.

For an instant she thought he was Carlos. Then a woman appeared, and he spoke to her, and Sophie saw that he had terrible teeth with gold fillings, and he wore an ostentatious gold watch and several rings. He was not like Carlos at all.

If I'm going to jump out of my skin every time I see a tall man with black hair, I shall soon be a nervous wreck, she thought, annoyed with herself.

A few minutes after five o'clock she drove through the entrance of the Torre del Moro camp ground where she was to live and work until the end of September.

"Sophie! We didn't expect to see you yet," exclaimed the blonde young woman who had been pinning up a poster advertising *flamenco* dancing as Sophie approached the reception kiosk.

"Hello, Margriet. How are you? You don't mind my arriving a day or two early, I hope?"

"Not at all – the sooner the better. There's plenty to be done, although as you will have noticed the camp is not very full yet," said Margriet Veenveld, in her excellent English. "Ah, here comes Piet."

Like his wife, Piet Veenveld, the camp manager, was fair-haired and blue-eyed. He had grown a thick, curly beard since Sophie had last seen him, and he was wearing a gay pair of Bermuda shorts. A CND medallion dangled against his muscular chest. In spite of their natural colouring, both he and Margriet were already deeply tanned.

"Sophie, it's good to see you. Did you enjoy the journey? How do you like Spain so far? I expect you are tired, eh? Sit down, and I'll get you a drink."

"What I need is exercise, Piet, not more sitting down. I'm longing for a swim. Is it possible?"

"Certainly. Margriet, take her up to the pool. I will look after things here."

"There's a beach on the other side of the hill for the campers, but we are allowed to use the private swimming pool up there when no one is staying at the *torre*," explained Margriet, accompanying Sophie to the car to fetch her bathing things.

She pointed to the massive old watch-tower on the headland overlooking the camp. "It belongs to a Marqués and his family, but I think it is only one of their summer houses. Last summer they were here for a few days in May, and later some friends of theirs were in residence for two weeks. The rest of the time it was empty."

As Sophie unlocked the car, the Dutch girl added, "You can change in your caravan. It's small. I hope you won't find it too small for comfort. It's in a nice shady position, and not too near the apartments. In the high season we have a lot of complaints from the campers about the noise from the apartments. Sometimes there are parties until two and three o'clock in the morning, and the campers become very annoyed because most of them like to go to bed early and to wake up early."

Sophie's first impression of her accommodation was that

while it might have been somewhat confined for the married couple who had helped the Veenvelds to run the camp the previous season, the caravan provided more than enough space for a single occupant.

As soon as she had changed, the two girls walked up the stony path which led over the headland to the beach used by the campers. On the inland side of the Moorish tower from which the camp took its name, an area of ground had been enclosed by a high, whitewashed wall. Taking a key from her beach bag, Margriet unlocked a thick iron-studded door in the wall, and gestured for the other girl to enter. The scene which met Sophie's eyes would have elicited a wordless exclamation of delight in any circumstances, and the fact that she was hot and travel-weary accentuated her reaction.

"Oh, Margriet . . . how heavenly!" she murmured, gazing in enchanted astonishment at the white-tiled octagonal pool of glass-smooth, sky-reflecting water in the centre of the flowery, leafy *patio*. All the shrubs and plants were growing from large pots arranged in groups on the colourful tile-paved floor. From the centre of the pool rose a plinth supporting a small but elaborate fountain. When Margriet pressed a switch hidden among the greenery on the wall, seven jets tossed sparkling plumes of water high into the sunlit air, and the three shallow basins began to spill rainbow fringes.

"If this were my home, I should live here all the year," remarked Margriet, half an hour later. They were sitting on the edge of the pool, dangling their legs in the water, and watching the fountain play. "But perhaps their other houses are even more attractive than this one."

"What is it like inside?" asked Sophie, studying the tower.

"Full of wonderful furniture and pictures, and beautiful
49

old rugs from the Alpujarra region on the other side of the hills between the coast and the city of Granada," answered Margriet. "The tower is air-conditioned so that if July and August are very humid nothing will be damaged by mildew. There's a gardener who comes every morning to look after the plants, and a woman who keeps the house ready. The Marqués must be very rich. Imagine being married to someone like that!"

"Is he married?" Sophie asked.

"Oh, yes, he has four or five children. The Marquesa is young and very attractive. But he is much older. He is short and quite fat, and –" she searched for a word "– and bald. So I think I prefer to live with Piet in a caravan."

Sophie had supper with the Veenvelds that evening. As they would not allow her to help wash the dishes afterwards, she sat in a deckchair outside the caravan from where she could see the moonlit *torre del Moro* which had guarded the headland for so many centuries.

The next day she started work. She spent the first morning following Piet round the camp, and meeting the local staff including the young Spanish husband and wife who cleaned the ablutions, old Pepe, the gardener-cum-dustman, the people who ran the camp shops, and the cook, barman and waiters at the camp restaurant.

In the afternoon, while Piet went up to the private pool to swim and snooze, Sophie sat in the reception kiosk with Margriet and learned about some of the campers' problems she would have to handle. In the early evening Margriet took her to Almuñecar, the nearest town of any size, to see the nightly *paseo* when all the local people who were not still at work strolled about the streets to see and be seen.

By the end of a week, she had mastered the routine work, although she still had difficulty in understanding anyone with a strong Andalusian accent.

She had been at the camp for three weeks when the wo-man who cleaned the tower told Margriet that some friends of the Marqués were arriving that evening, and staying for two nights, during which time the Veenvelds and the Eng-lish *señorita* would have to swim from the beach.

The following morning, Sophie set out for her now cus-tomary pre-breakfast swim. Piet and Margriet did not care for the beach which soon, they said, would be impossibly crowded, and which even in its uncrowded state consisted of fine grey grit merging into shingle where it shelved quick-ly into deep water.

Sophie had to concede that the colour and texture of the beach would come as a shock to anyone expecting the Costa del Sol to boast mile upon mile of powder-fine golden sand, and also that the shape of the foreshore in the bay made it somewhat unsuitable for children and timid bathers. But as far as she was concerned, the transparency of the Mediter-ranean, and the fascination of fish-watching with the aid of a mask and snorkel, made up for any other deficiencies. Also she liked the beach bar with tables and chairs set out in a fenced enclosure under a shady *esparto* canopy. The beach bar was run by an Englishman called Mike who was pleasant enough to the campers, but no more than civil to the Veenvelds or Sophie.

As she passed the door of the walled garden that mor-ning, she heard the sound of splashing from within. It was not the rhythmic sibilance of the fountains. Checking her pace for a moment, she heard a girlish squeak of mock-alarm, followed by a masculine laugh and a further flurry of violent splashing. Sophie smiled. Perhaps the Marqués's guests were honeymooners.

As she paused there, sensing the carefree happiness of the couple sporting in the pool, she was suddenly assailed by a sharp pang of her own unhappiness. She had managed to

51

hide it from Piet and Margriet, and she tried not to think about it herself, but sometimes it caught her unawares.

At this hour of the morning Mike's bar was shuttered and padlocked. The beach was deserted except for the scrawny white mule which sometimes, to Sophie's concern, was tethered there without shade or water.

At the sight of her, the creature began to bray, its raucous cries reverberated between the rocky headlands. She hushed it with bread and carrots. A few moments later she was floating, face down, in the warm sea, watching a shoal of striped fish.

When she went swimming before breakfast she did not take a towel or a robe. No one else was about, and it had become her habit, on returning, to go directly to the shower house, there to rinse the salt from her hair and skin with fresh water pumped from the deep wells which also supplied the camp's drinking water.

This morning as she came out of the sea, she pushed her green rubber face mask up over her hair. Then she scrambled up the slope of loose shingle to where she had left her rubber sand shoes. She put them on, and began to trudge up the beach, watching the mule and wondering who was its owner.

"Momento, señorita, por favor!"

The curt request, coming from the rocks above her, startled her. But a second, greater shock was to come. The man who was frowning down at her from a ledge of rock about thirty feet above the beach was Carlos Walsingham.

For some moments Sophie was tongue-tied. While she was standing there, paralysed with astounded dismay, Carlos picked his way down the steep face of the promontory. He jumped the last few feet, and landed less than two yards from her.

"So we meet again," he said coldly. "I didn't expect to

52

find you here. But surprises are your speciality, aren't they? You turn up unexpectedly, and you vanish even more unexpectedly."

She began to recover herself. "My departure from the Hotel Miramar may have been unexpected to you. I don't think it would have surprised most people. I happen to understand Spanish, and I didn't care for the tone of your conversation about me with Señor Garcia. You were mistaken in assuming that I was 'throwing' myself at you with a view to 'enjoying your generosity' for as long as I could hold your interest. I am not a toy, Mr. Walsingham, and I don't like men who regard girls in that light."

As she made to brush past him, Carlos caught her by the forearm. "Why didn't you tell me this at the time? It would have been more sensible than disappearing without a word of explanation."

"Were you worried?" Sophie asked cuttingly. "Did you scour the countryside searching for me?"

"Naturally I looked for you. Did you suppose that when I discovered you had gone I shrugged my shoulders and left it at that?"

"It wouldn't surprise me. Would you take your hand off my arm, please?"

"Very well, but don't try to walk away, because I will stop you."

Sophie gave an expressive grimace. "And you ask me why I left the Miramar without an explanation!"

She had the satisfaction of seeing that this thrust had hit home. Now he knew how she had felt, listening to the exchange between him and Jorge Garcia.

But although for an instant his jaw clenched, and his grey eyes were momentarily fierce, his anger died down as swiftly as it had flared. "Do you seriously expect me to believe that you thought I would force myself on you even if you

53

told me my attentions were unwelcome?"

"I had already had one unpleasant eye-opener. I didn't feel inclined to risk a worse one."

A movement among the rocks above them, and a flash of bright colour, made them both glance upwards. A young girl was clambering down to join them. She had long black hair plaited in a single lustrous pigtail, and her arms and legs were the coffee colour of olive skin when it is tanned, rather than the amber shade of Sophie's limbs. The girl was wearing yellow shorts, and a white tee-shirt with a large sunflower head printed on the front of it.

As she reached the rock from which Carlos had leapt, he went to help her down. Crouching, she laid her hands on his broad shoulders. With an easy swing, he transferred her from the rock to the shingle.

"*Buenos días, señorita.*" The girl smiled at Sophie, and bobbed.

She was tall, but not more than twelve. The sunflower adorned a chest almost as flat as a boy's, yet there was nothing of the tomboy about her. She wore tiny pearls in her pierced ears, and there was colourless polish on her short but well-kept fingernails. It was only a matter of time before her figure caught up with the already remarkable beauty of her face.

Carlos introduced her. "Mari-Luz is the eldest daughter of the owners of the tower. This is Miss Lingwood, *chica*."

"How do you do, Miss Lingwood," the girl said, in English, holding out her hand.

Sophie shook hands. Then she turned to Carlos, and said briskly, "I must go or I shall be late for breakfast. In any case there is nothing further to discuss. Goodbye, *señor*."

The '*señor*' slipped out, perhaps because he was so very Spanish-looking, perhaps because it seemed to emphasise the antipathy he aroused in her now, and also the finality of her 'Goodbye.'

After breakfast Piet sent her to bank some money in Almuñecar. When she returned there was an influx of new arrivals to be settled in.

It was not until lunchtime that Margriet remembered she had some news for the other two. "We've been invited to have dinner up at the *torre* tonight, Piet. One of the people staying there is Carlos Walsingham. He was in the camp for a short time this morning, but he could see it was a busy spell so he didn't stay long. You are included in the invitation, Sophie. I explained to him that the Kuypers were not helping us this year because Sonja is expecting a baby, and I told him about Sophie and the young man who is coming next week. Carlos asked many questions about you, Sophie. He is a very attractive man. You two could have fun together, I think."

"I met Mr. Walsingham on the beach this morning. I don't like him," said Sophie flatly. "I'm allergic to men of his type. I don't want to come to the dinner party, Margriet. You can easily say I have a headache or toothache, or something."

The Dutch girl looked amazed. "Sophie, you can't mean that? No girl could dislike Carlos. I find him charming. If he has already met you, it explains his curiosity about you. He did not seem at all interested in Sacha, but clearly you have made a good impression on him."

"I'm sure you're mistaken, Margriet. But anyway, *I* don't like *him*, and I don't want to meet him again."

"That makes a rather difficult situation, Sophie," said Piet, looking thoughtfully at her. "You see, Carlos Walsingham is the owner of this camp. It's probably the least important and profitable of his various enterprises, but last year he made several unexpected visits to check that the place was running smoothly. Usually he stays in Almuñecar,

55

not at the *torre,* although he is related to the Marqués."

"*He* owns the camp? I thought it belonged to the Marqués."

"No, no, only the *torre* and the land around it is the property of the Marqués. The rest belongs to Carlos Walsingham, including the holiday apartments most of which are rented by people from Granada."

"Which means that Carlos is our boss," put in Margriet. "And one does not wish to offend the boss if it can be avoided. Whatever you feel about him personally, Sophie, it would be foolish to miss a good dinner, and the opportunity to see all the beautiful things inside the *torre.* There are many books," she added, knowing something of Sophie's interest in fine bindings and rare volumes.

It was not this last inducement however which made Sophie change her mind, but the awareness that Margriet and Piet were genuinely worried about the possibility of offending the man who was the source of their income.

Later, she said to Margriet, "You do have a contract, presumably? Carlos Walsingham couldn't sack you on the strength of a whim?"

"Oh, yes, we have a contract, and I am sure he is a man who would not break an unwritten agreement unless he had a very good reason," answered the Dutch girl. "But if he is pleased with us as managers at the end of our second season here, who knows what he may offer Piet? We both want to stay in Spain. Holland is becoming too crowded, and the weather is not good. You know how it is, Sophie. It is very much the same in England."

"Mm, but in spite of the often dreary weather, there are many things about England which I should miss if I had to give them up permanently. And the Costa del Sol isn't exactly under-populated," said Sophie dryly. For now the Torre del Moro camp was full, and the two most recently-arrived families were having to camp in the dust of the car park until spaces in the camp proper became available.

It was half past nine when Piet and the two girls walked up the path to the *torre*. Piet had put on a suit, and Margriet had had her hair done at the *peluqueria* on the ground floor of the apartment block, and was wearing a frilly evening blouse, a long flower-splashed skirt, and a good deal of sparkling jewellery. They had both looked rather doubtfully at Sophie's plain dress of white cotton gaberdine with which she wore scarlet leather slippers and a long gold muff chain looped twice round her neck. Her handkerchief and lipstick were inside a small red coin purse. Her hair was held at the nape of her neck by a discreet tortoiseshell clasp.

There was no one in the moonlit courtyard when Piet pushed open the door in the wall, and stood aside for the girls to precede him. But when he rapped on the door of the tower, there was only a brief interval before it was opened by Mari-Luz who welcomed them into a semi-circular hall from which a stone staircase followed the curve of the outer wall to the floor above. As the Spanish child led the way to the first floor *sala*, Sophie realised that when the tower had been converted into a house, a new wall had been erected along the diameter. On the seaward side of this were the rooms, while the inland side was occupied by a tier of galleries connected by crescent flights of stairs. Both the stairs and the galleries were guarded by magnificent wrought iron balustrades.

From the camp, as from the beach, the tower appeared to have only a few small and heavily barred windows. But when Sophie walked into the *sala* she saw that on the seaward side the thick wall had been pierced by a larger window, invisible to anyone looking at the tower from the land.

The window, with a general impression of rich colours and texture, was all that she had time to notice before Car-

57

los walked forward to shake hands with her, and to present her to an elegant elderly woman who, to Sophie's surprise, he introduced as Mrs. McKinlay.

It was not until they went down to dinner in the ground floor dining-room that Sophie learned the reason why, in spite of her Scottish surname, Mrs. McKinlay looked and dressed like a Frenchwoman, but was known to Carlos as Tía Jacinta.

While the two men were discussing the management of the camp, and Margriet was conversing with Mari-Luz, Mrs. McKinlay turned to Sophie and said, "Carlos tells me this is your first visit to Spain, Miss Lingwood, but that you have a good command of the language. How does that come about?"

Sophie explained, adding, "But I have great difficulty in understanding the Andalusian accent."

A reminiscent twinkle came into Mrs. McKinlay's large dark eyes. "I had the same difficulty many years ago when I was first married. My sisters and I had had an English-woman among our several governesses, but for a long time after my marriage I found it impossible to understand the Scots accents of the staff at my mother-in-law's home near Dundee."

"I should imagine you found it rather hard to accustom yourself to the Scottish climate, didn't you?"

"I expect I should have done so, had we lived there. But my husband was in the Diplomatic Service, and our first home together was in China. My husband is retired now, of course, and after a lifetime of travelling we are inclined to stay put in our quiet corner of Scotland. However last winter was exceptionally severe, and a few weeks ago, when it was still very chilly, I suddenly felt a great longing to see Andalusia in the spring once more. At present we're stay-ing with Mari-Luz's parents. When Carlos arrived and mentioned that he was driving right along the coast from San Pedro to Motril, I thought it would be interesting to see for myself the great change brought about by *turismo*. My husband felt the trip would be too tiring for him, so dear little Mari-Luz offered to come and keep me company when Carlos is busy with matters of business."

"Is Mari-Luz your granddaughter?"

"No, my great-niece. Her mother is one of my youngest sister's children, and her father and Carlos's mother are cousins. The ramifications of Spanish families are very complex," she added, smiling. "Are you part of a large family, Miss Lingwood?"

Sophie was about to explain why she was an only child when she changed her mind, and said only, "No, I'm not."

It went against the grain with her to be uncommunicative with someone she liked. But she felt sure that any information she imparted to Mrs. McKinlay would eventually reach Carlos, and as far as he was concerned she wished to maintain an impenetrable reserve.

"What part of England do you come from?" enquired Mrs. McKinlay.

"Sussex." Sophie side-stepped further questions by asking the older woman which country, of those she had lived in during her husband's diplomatic career, she had liked best.

Coffee was taken in the *sala*, and not long afterwards Mari-Luz said goodnight.

"Would you like to see my room, Miss Lingwood?" she asked.

She was so eager to show it that Sophie could not refuse. There were three adult bedrooms on the floor above the *sala*, and two dormitories for children on the third floor.

"I want to sleep on the roof, but Tío Carlos will not allow it," Mari-Luz said regretfully. "I wish we came here

59

more often. I like to swim, but the others like to ride."

"How is it that you aren't at school?" asked Sophie.

"We are taught at home by Mademoiselle St. Just. My brother Joaquin goes to school in Switzerland, and Esteban will go when he is thirteen. But Mama thinks it is best for girls to stay at home. Did you go to school, Miss Lingwood?"

"Yes, but not to a boarding school. I attended a day school in the town where I grew up. May I look at your books?" – indicating a built-in fitment for books and toys.

The children's rooms were the only part of the *torre* which had been appointed and furnished in a modern manner.

From the hall to the highest landing, the wall of the tower was exposed in its original state. In the *sala*, the stonework was hidden by plaster. In the children's rooms, varnished pine panelling and bunk beds created an informal, boat-like atmosphere.

While Mari-Luz prepared for bed, chattering as she did so, Sophie cast a practised eye along the several shelves of what a book dealer would classify as 'juveniles'. It was a heterogeneous collection. Asterix and Tin-tin rubbed shoulders with Paddington and Mr. Bumblemoose, Charles Perrault with Richmal Crompton, Cervantes with Henty.

Inside an Edwardian copy of *Winning the Golden Spurs, or Raoul and Iron Hand, a Tale of the 14th Century,* Sophie found a home-made book-plate incorporating the words 'From the library of Carlos James Walsingham.'

A slight frown contracted her eyebrows. Had Carlos been bookish as a schoolboy? Had she given the matter any thought, she would have supposed him to have been too restless and energetic a boy to care for reading as a pastime.

There was a knock on the door.

Mari-Luz called, "*Adelante!*"

Carlos walked into the room.

"I thought you might like to see the view from the roof, Sophie. Mari-Luz will come with us. You will be in no danger," he added, with a gleam of mockery.

"Oh, yes, you needn't be nervous," the child assured her. "The *parapeto* makes it impossible to fall."

The roof was reached by a steep flight of wooden steps at the other end of the landing. The trapdoor was locked and bolted. When he had undone it, Carlos pushed it upwards and climbed out on to the roof. Then he turned to offer a helping hand to Sophie.

"Thank you." As quickly as possible she disengaged her fingers and moved away.

From this height the block of apartments overlooking the camp seemed quite a small building. In the opposite direction it was possible to see the clustered lights of Almuñecar in the distance.

"The stone is still warm," murmured Sophie presently, resting her forearms on the top of the parapet, and gazing down at the calm sea far below.

Beside her, Mari-Luz was star-gazing, her long hair, no longer plaited, flowing over her shoulders. Her nightdress was ankle-length, the soft folds of leaf-scattered voile falling from a pin-tucked yoke edge with lace round the neck and armholes.

"*Why* won't you let me sleep up here, Tío?" she asked. "What could happen to me?"

"Nothing, but I don't think your parents would approve; and as you didn't rest this afternoon – which I *know* would not please your mother – it is high time you were in bed, *chica.*"

Mari-Luz did not argue. "Goodnight, Miss Lingwood."

But Sophie had no intention of being left on the tower roof with Carlos. "We had better come down too, I think."

61

She returned to the trapdoor.

On the landing outside her room, the child shook hands with Sophie and repeated the engaging bob she had given that morning. Then Carlos bent his tall head, and she stood on tiptoe to kiss his cheek. In Spanish, she said mischievously, "The last one in the pool tomorrow morning is bradypodida choloepus."

"I didn't understand the last bit," said Sophie, when Mari-Luz had whisked into her bedroom, and they were descending the staircase.

"Bradypodida choloepus is the two-toed sloth."

"Oh, I see." She forced herself to move briskly but calmly. To hurry too much would be to ask for trouble.

Somewhat to her surprise, he made no attempt to resume their interrupted exchange on the beach, but walked down the stairs in silence. But she felt him watching her, and she was sure that he knew she had not wished to come to dinner, and that he was amused by the contrast between her manner towards him tonight and her unguarded warmth in Barcelona.

On the gallery outside the *sala*, he said, "If you would care to join our pre-breakfast water sports, you are very welcome."

"Thank you, but I really prefer sea bathing." With relief she entered the *sala*.

Her relaxation was temporary, however, as the only person there was Mrs. McKinlay who, wearing a pair of horn-rimmed spectacles, was embroidering a piece of fine linen stretched in a tambour frame.

"The Veenvelds had to leave early," she explained, removing her spectacles. "A messenger came up from the camp to say there was trouble brewing at the *discoteca*. Nothing very serious, I fancy. No doubt Piet will soon put matters right."

"I had better go. I may be needed," said Sophie, at once.

"No, don't go yet," said Mrs. McKinlay. "He didn't want his wife to go with him, but she insisted. I suspect that she had a headache, and was glad of the excuse. Carlos, I should like some of that special Madeira, and perhaps Miss Lingwood would like to try it, too. Come and sit down, my dear" – patting the sofa beside her, and replacing her spectacles. "You won't mind if I carry on with my work, I hope? I'm doing a set of napkins for a wedding present, and I am rather behind schedule with them."

Sitting beside her, Sophie was able to see that the older woman was engaged in some very beautiful lace-like pulled work. Something about the design rang a bell in her mind, and after a few moments' thought, she said, "You are not the Mrs. McKinlay who worked that incredible tablecloth for the last Country Women of the World competition, are you?"

Mrs. McKinlay looked startled. "Yes, I am. How did you know about the cloth?"

"There was a photograph of it in *Embroidery*. Something about the motif you're doing now reminded me of it."

For the second time, Mrs. McKinlay took off her glasses. "What a delightful surprise," she said, smiling. "I had no idea I was talking to a fellow member of the Guild. Somehow – quite wrongly, I daresay – one thinks of embroiderers as middle-aged or elderly people, never as girls of your age."

"I don't belong to the Embroiderers' Guild," Sophie corrected her. "But the aunt who brought me up is a member, so I see the Guild's magazine, and I know a good deal about emdroidery. My aunt is Rose Steel," she added, forgetting her resolve to keep Carlos, and everyone connected with him, at arm's length.

"Oh, you fortunate creature! How I wish Rose Steel was

63

a member of my family," exclaimed Mrs. McKinlay excitedly. "I think she is by far the most brilliant embroiderer at work today, and her splendid book *The Past, Present and Future of Embroidery* is a constant refreshment to me. I do so agree with her view that needlework at its finest is always functional as well as beautiful. I'm very impatient of the recent floodtide of experimental 'hangings' which are said to be so creative, but which I think are merely undisciplined. In embroidery, as in everything else, one must learn the rules first, and *then* break them. Ah, thank you, Carlos" – as he placed a glass of pale amber wine on the table at her end of the sofa.

"Thank you." Sophie took the glass he handed to her.

As she answered Mrs. McKinlay's questions about her aunt, she was conscious of Carlos's scrutiny, and the knowledge that he would probably insist on escorting her down the hill path sent a tremor of apprehension through her.

"Poor Carlos, are you very bored by all this chatter about embroidery?" asked Mrs. McKinlay presently.

"Not at all. How could I be bored with two pretty women to look at?"

Mrs. McKinlay laughed. "There speaks the son of Mercedes! The thoroughly British male is not adept at paying compliments."

"Have you nothing to say in defence of your countrymen, Sophie?" Carlos asked, looking at her with the smile in his eyes which in Barcelona she had liked, but which now – knowing there was no real warmth of heart behind that look – she disliked and resented.

"I agree: they are not good at being gallant. But I think that's largely because the British female doesn't attach much importance to pretty speeches. So often a man who says and does charming things is not nearly so nice and worthwhile as the type of man who is hopeless at making gallant gestures and murmuring sweet nothings."

"Yes, too much charm can be a bad sign," agreed Mrs. McKinlay. "On the other hand, I'm suspicious of men who can never bring themselves to say anything nice to a woman, and whose gifts are always practical things. If Ninian had ever presented me with a set of saucepans – which I have known to happen to some wives – I should have thrown one at him and the rest out of the window. Happily for me, my husband is very good at choosing presents which please me. This was for my last birthday. Isn't it pretty?" – showing Sophie her gold thimble, and the carved ivory case in which it fitted.

When Sophie said she must go, Mrs. McKinlay accompanied her down the stairs to the hall.

"Do tell your aunt what great pleasure her book has given me," she said. "She's extraordinarily versatile, isn't she? One of the colour plates is of a canvas-work stool top which is quite different in technique and design from anything else in the book."

"Well, church embroideries are her professional speciality but privately she enjoys every type of embroidery. I think cut-work is her only blind spot. Just before I left England, she gave me an evening cloak with the most lovely beaded hood."

"Did you bring it with you?"

"Yes."

"Oh, I should love to see it. Is that possible?"

From behind them, Carlos suggested, "Why don't you have lunch together tomorrow? I shall be out all day," he added, rather sardonically, as Sophie glanced over her shoulder at him.

"I'm on duty at lunchtime tomorrow," she told Mrs. McKinlay. "But if you wouldn't mind visiting the camp during the morning, I'd be glad to show the cloak to you."

"Of course, my dear. I shall be interested to see the camp at close quarters. Would ten o'clock be convenient for you?"

"Ten would be fine. Thank you for a most enjoyable evening."

Having shaken hands with Mrs. McKinlay, Sophie thought she might as well *try* to escape the ordeal which she sensed lay ahead of her.

"If you are going to offer to walk down with me, it is really quite unnecessary, Mr. Walsingham. The moonlight makes it easy to see the path. In two minutes I shall be there."

"You may not need my escort, Miss Lingwood, but nevertheless my Spanish ancestors would turn in their graves if I did not insist on seeing you safely to your door," Carlos answered blandly. And to Sophie's greater alarm, he turned to the older woman, saying, "I expect you will have gone to bed before I return, Tia. Goodnight. Sleep well." He raised her hand to his lips.

In the courtyard, following Sophie round the edge of the motionless pool, he said, "I am aware that there was a time when it was not unusual for women to address their husbands as Mr. So-and-so. But don't you think it's a little absurd to call me Mr. Walsingham when, not very long ago, you allowed me to kiss you?"

"I didn't know then that you were to be my employer."

"I'm not. Piet is your employer."

"You own the camp. You are his boss."

They had reached the door in the wall, but instead of opening it, Carlos touched the switch which brought the fountain to life. Unwilling to linger, but unable to ignore anything so beautiful, Sophie watched the shining jets splinter into a thousand diamond drops.

"In fact my being, indirectly, your boss has nothing to do with all this stiff-necked formality, has it?" said Carlos

66

dryly. "What rankles is that unfortunate conversation between me and Jorge Garcia. I wonder what would have happened if you hadn't heard it, or had heard it but not understood it?"

"The outcome would have been the same, the only difference being that I should have left the Miramar later than I did, and spent the night somewhere other than where I did spend it."

"But perhaps you wouldn't have found it necessary to leave at all. No, wait a moment. Hear me out."

As she turned to open the door, he stretched out his arm and spread his left hand on the woodwork. It was only a symbolic gesture, but she guessed he would have no scruples about holding the door shut by real force if necessary.

"I haven't much choice," she said, shrugging.

"Suppose we had dined at the Carlton Hotel in Alicante, and then we had danced for an hour or two, after which I had taken you back to the Miramar and begun to make love to you. Would you really have left the hotel then? At two o'clock in the morning? Or would you have said firmly 'No', and locked your door, and gone to bed alone, but not really angry with me? I think, if you have the courage to be honest, you will admit that's what would have happened – if you hadn't been able to speak Spanish."

She said, in a low voice, "Very well, I will be honest with you. Perhaps that is what would have happened. But I should still have left the hotel early the next morning, before you were up. And I should still have hoped not to meet you again."

"Sophie, we are living in the 1970s, not the 1870s. I am not obtuse: I have grasped the fact that you are not a disciple of the so-called permissive society. But with your face and your figure, you will never convince me that I'm the first man who has ever made a pass at you – or rather who

67

intended to make one, given a little more time," he added, with sardonic humour.

"I didn't say you were."

"You behaved as though I was ... or would have been."

"I thought ... I expected you to be different."

"Why?" he said blankly.

"Because ... oh, I don't know why. Haven't you ever hoped that some day, somewhere, somebody will like you for yourself? Not because you're the rich Carlos Walsingham. Not because you're tall and dark and attractive. Just because of something inside you which —" To her horror, her voice became husky and tears blurred her vision. "I'm tired, and I have to be up early. Please let me go, Carlos."

He opened the door and stood aside. In silence, they walked down the hill until she was calm enough to say, "Anyway, that was *not* the way it happened. And if you were a girl, and not a promiscuous one, I daresay you wouldn't take kindly to be lined up for the Walsingham harem on less than twenty-four hours' acquaintance."

"The Walsingham harem? What are you talking about?"

"I can't pretend I wasn't warned," she said bitterly. "Mrs. Hellington told me you were a pasha. But I, like an idiot, ignored her."

Carlos laughed. "Pashas are Turkish. The harem is an Arab institution. The next time you see Mrs. Hellington you can tell her that it's true that I'm supposed to have the blood of Moulay Abu Hassan in my veins. Unfortunately it has been very much diluted by five hundred years of marriage to assorted Christians, and I lack his remarkable vitality. Had you joined my harem, *querida*, you would have been its only occupant."

"You may not have as *many* women. You obviously have precisely the same attitude to them."

68

"Until we met at the Miramar, you seemed to find my attitude acceptable."

"I didn't realise what you had in mind. You seemed ... I thought –"

"You intrigue me," Carlos said softly, when she fell silent. "If you didn't realise that I hoped we might have a pleasant time together, you must have believed I was serious. *Did* you think that?"

"I – I don't know. It seemed ... a possibility."

It was then that she trod on a loose stone, and swayed, and perhaps would have overbalanced if he had not caught her and drawn her to him.

"It still is a possibility – if you stop being angry with me. I can't fall in love with a girl who doesn't want to know me."

He tilted her face up to his. Behind his dark head the moonlit watch-tower loomed against a backcloth of stars. For an instant, held in his arms, so close that she could feel his heart beating, the memory of all her schoolgirl fantasies about him were suddenly so overpoweringly real that all resistance went out of her.

It was only a momentary weakness. Almost immediately she stiffened, and wrenched herself free. "I don't think serious relationships are your style. If they were, Señor Garcia wouldn't have made that remark about your being determined to keep your freedom. You're no more interested in me as a person now than you were before. My face and figure pass muster. My mind you couldn't care less about."

She paused for breath and, when Carlos didn't contradict her, went on, "The only reason you still remember my name is because I'm probably the first girl who's ever walked out and left you looking foolish in front of an associate. Goodnight."

And she turned and hurried the rest of the way to the camp.

On her way to the shower house next morning, she passed Mike from the beach bar. He lived in a tiny caravan in a corner of the camp, but he was not usually an early riser.

"Hi, Sophie." He gave her a friendly nod.

While she was brushing her teeth, Margriet strolled in, yawning, and dumped her plastic toilet bag on the ledge at the back of the basin. "You're up early, Sophie. I thought you would sleep late this morning. What time did you come home?"

"About midnight."

Sophie enquired about the trouble at the *discoteca,* and Margriet shrugged and told her that by the time Piet appeared on the scene the small disturbance had blown over.

"Mrs. McKinlay thought you had a headache last night. Did you?"

The Dutch girl grinned. "No! I was being tactful, giving Carlos the chance to walk in the moonlight with you. Do you like him better now?"

"Your tact was wasted, Margriet. He's just not my type." Sophie pulled on her shower cap, and disappeared inside one of the cubicles opposite the long row of handbasins.

Punctually at ten o'clock, Mrs. McKinlay and Mari-Luz arrived at the reception kiosk. Mari-Luz was delighted with Sophie's living quarters.

"I wish I could work here all summer, and live in a *caravana* like this one," she said, with an envious sigh. "We are leaving this evening. As soon as Tío Carlos has finished some business in Almuñecar, we are going to Granada to visit Tío Eduardo and Tía Giselda."

While Mari-Luz admired the caravan, Mrs. McKinlay gloated over the embroidery on the hood of the sea-green cloak.

It was Sophie's afternoon off that day, and she spent it fish-watching. Between swims, she sat in the beach bar enclosure, sipping Fanta orangeade, and chatting to Mike who was in a more sociable mood than usual.

When she returned to the camp Margriet told her that Carlos had been to say goodbye, and had asked for Sophie. "I told him you were at the beach. Did he find you?"

"No, I didn't see him. I was in the sea most of the time."

Privately, Sophie doubted if Carlos had been near the beach. She felt sure that her remark about him looking a fool in front of Señor Garcia would rankle as much, if not more, than the thought of being taken for one of his casual amours had rankled with her.

Oddly, instead of feeling pleased and relieved that she was free of his unsettling presence, she spent the evening in a mood of unreasonable depression.

After supper, she wrote to her aunt, telling her about Mrs. McKinlay, but omitting any reference to Carlos. Then she went to bed early and read Washington Irving's account of *The Legend of the Three Beautiful Princesses*. The book was too old and valuable to take to the beach, and she had read very little of it since her arrival at the camp.

Her first concern had been to polish her Spanish by reading the local newspaper and Spanish magazines from which she could pick up current idioms and vogue words.

The legend of the princesses was interesting because, while most of the action took place in the Alhambra at Granada, which Sophie intended to visit on the first of her three-day breaks, the story began in the ancient castle at Salobreña which was only a few kilometres from the camp, and which she had noticed when she was driving along the coast road.

Even in the pages of a century-and-a-half-old travel book she could not escape thoughts of Carlos Walsingham. The three Moorish princesses had fallen in love with three Spanish prisoners of war, and presently Sophie read a passage which perfectly described her own predicament.

"– *the difficulties of their intercourse added to its charms,
and strengthened the passion they had so singularly con-
ceived for love delights to struggle with difficulties, and
thrives the most hardily on the scantiest soil.*"

No soil could possibly be scantier than the basis of her
relationship with Carlos, she thought, with a heavy sigh.
Her feelings for him were like weeds surviving on bare rock.
The episode at the Miramar had not really withered them,
although pride made her try to convince herself that it had
done so. Even now, when she felt she had been successful
in killing his transient interest in her, she had not truly
hardened her heart against him. Instead of being glad that
she was unlikely to encounter him a fourth time, she felt
profoundly miserable.

CHAPTER THREE

THE following morning she received a short letter from Kate Dilham whose villa-minding job on the Costa Brava was exceeding her expectations, and a long letter from Grandplum. Considering that he was in his late seventies, and for several years past had seldom set foot outside Cliff Court, Mr. Lingwood was an entertaining correspondent.

At noon, Piet and Margriet went up to the *torre* to swim, leaving Sophie on duty at the kiosk. The camp was already full, with three families making the best of spaces in the car park. Thus any new arrivals would have to be directed to a rival camp on the far side of Almuñecar.

Sophie was adding a page to the letter she had written the night before, when someone said, *"Buenos días,"* and she looked up from her writing case to find a young man with a piratical moustache smiling at her. A guitar in a canvas bag was slung over his shoulder, and he was wearing an embroidered Moroccan shirt and sun-bleached jeans. His feet were bare, but his fingers were adorned with several rings. He was the sort of young man to whom most people of Rose Steel's generation reacted with alarm or apoplexy. Sophie noticed that his hair, nails and clothes were clean, and her smile was as friendly for him as for anyone else.

Before she could ask how she could help him, he said, in French, "You puzzle me, beautiful girl. I can't guess your nationality. Perhaps you are like me – a mixture, eh?"

"I'm English. But I speak some French," she answered, in French.

"And I speak very good American, so we have no prob-

73

lems about communicating. I'm Sacha Lucien, the new help."

She blinked a little at this information. Most of the campers were middle-aged French, German and English people, with a sprinkling of Spaniards and Scandinavians. She had a feeling they might look askance at Sacha as a member of the camp staff. However, Piet had met him and liked him, so no doubt he had other talents besides playing a guitar.

"I'm Sophie Lingwood. Welcome to Torre del Moro. Have you come a long way? Are you hungry or thirsty, or both?"

"I wouldn't refuse some cold beer."

Piet had installed a small refrigerator under the counter. Sophie took out a bottle of San Miguel for Sacha, and a bottle of Fanta for herself. She put two clean tumblers on the counter, found the opener and deftly flipped off the bottle caps.

"I've come from Granada. Have you been there?" asked Sacha.

She shook her head. "Is the Alhambra as beautiful as they say?"

He shrugged. "I didn't see it. I don't like the tourist places. The road through the mountains, that's *fantastico*! I hitched a ride on a lorry, and we sang, and we ate *chorizo*. Do you like *chorizo*?"

"I haven't had very much."

He opened the small grip which seemed to be his only luggage apart from the guitar, and produced a long dark red sausage. From his pocket he took a curved Spanish clasp knife, cut an inch off the sausage, peeled it, and offered it to her on the point of the blade.

The red meat was marbled with white fat, and flavoured with garlic and paprika which made the juice a bright orange colour. The texture was chewy, some people would have

74

said tough. To Sophie, who had an adventurous palate, the taste was delicious, akin to salami but better.

Sacha taught Sophie many things about Spain in the course of his first week at the camp. Instead of travelling down the tourist coast, as she had done, he had hitch-hiked a leisurely way through central Spain, putting up at *posadas* the cheap, sometimes rough and ready, inns which originally had provided accommodation for muleteers, and now catered mainly to lorry drivers. In consequence, he had seen the real Spain behind the artificial façade of the holiday resorts, and his descriptions of hill villages and wild valleys made Sophie long to see them for herself.

In spite of his rings and embroidered shirts and bare feet, he quickly proved himself popular with even the most conventional-looking campers. The only person who refused to warm to him was Mike, who referred to him as "that damned hippy character."

"I like him. He's clean and kind and cheerful. What have you got against him?" asked Sophie, the first time she heard Mike refer to Sacha in this way.

"I've no time for these young drop-outs, swanning around Europe in fancy dress, smoking pot and generally making a nuisance of themselves."

"Sacha doesn't smoke anything," said Sophie, eyeing the cigarette between Mike's kipper-coloured forefingers. "He's working for a living. I think his clothes are fun, and his hair is no longer than yours."

And cleaner, she added mentally. For Mike, like some Spaniards, used pomade on his hair.

One day Sacha asked Sophie if she would care to spend the evening in Almuñecar with him. When she mentioned to Margriet that he was taking her to supper at the Vizcaya Bar which had a reputation for good food, the Dutch girl said, "Oh, so he does like girls. I wasn't sure about him. He doesn't seem the effeminate type, but he doesn't watch you when you are not looking, Sophie. Do you find *him* attractive?"

"I don't know. I haven't thought about him in that way. I like him as a person."

"Has he told you about himself? When I have asked him about his family, he tells crazy stories and I know he is joking with me."

"Perhaps, like me, he is merely having a fling before he settles down," suggested Sophie. "He may come from an extremely respectable, dull family, and in a year or two he may sell his guitar and become as respectable and dull as his father."

"If you are having a fling, it is not a very wild one," remarked Margriet quizzically. "You weren't interested in Carlos, and you haven't noticed that Sacha is a good-looking boy. What kind of man do you like? Don't tell me Mike is your type?"

"Heavens, no!" said Sophie emphatically. "I'm not very keen to be emotionally involved with anyone yet, Margriet. Ideally, I'd like to stay single until I'm about twenty-five."

But if Carlos had been as I imagined him, I would have married him at once, she thought, with a pang.

When Sacha came to her caravan that evening, he was wearing baseball boots, white drill loon pants, and an old but still colourful waistcoat of blue velvet embroidered with orange braid and gold sequins which he said he had bought in the Flea Market in Paris.

"I should think it's mid-nineteenth century Yugoslavian work," said Sophie, admiring it.

Guessing that his fancy dress, as Mike sneeringly called it, would be even more fancy than usual for an evening out, she had done her best to conform to his taste in clothes by teaming a melon-yellow tee-shirt with a pair of wide tur-

76

quoise pants, and linking them with a long, fringed Persian scarf would round her narrow waist.

They drove to Almuñecar in her car, which they parked in a side street before joining the evening *paseo* on the marble-paved promenade overlooking one of the town's twin beaches.

The centre of Almuñecar, where patient, panniered mules still clip-clopped up and down the steep-narrow streets, lay behind the ruins of an ancient fortress. On the seaward side of this hilltop castle stood the large crescent-shaped Hotel Sexi, commanding a view of both beaches.

The western beach served a recent eruption of tall, balconied blocks of flats, and a cluster of pre-boom summer villas which, no doubt, in time would have to make way for yet more apartments.

After strolling about the town for an hour or so, they made their way to the Vizcaya where, remembering the restaurant in Barcelona, Sophie smiled and said good evening to the people already dining. Sacha's colourful waistcoat and bare arms caused a good deal of comment among the Spaniards, and the waitress who took his order had difficulty in suppressing her giggles. But he seemed not to notice the sideways glances and nudges, and presently they paid less attention to him.

"You look sad, Sophie. Why?" he asked suddenly.

Quickly she pinned on a cheerful expression. She had been thinking about Barcelona and how, for a night and a day, she had lived in a fool's paradise. "That was my hungry expression," she answered lightly. "I'm looking forward to the swordfish steaks."

It was the first of many evenings together. In the month that followed, they sampled all the local eating places and *discotecas*. But although he sometimes called her 'beautiful girl', Sacha treated her more like a sister than a girl-friend.

He liked to dance, but only to energetic music. When the tempo slowed and the lights dimmed, he professed fatigue and a powerful thirst. He avoided holding her close in public, and he never attempted to do so in private. To Sophie, still deeply disturbed by her two encounters with Carlos, Sacha's attitude was a relief.

One afternoon when the beach was even more crowded than usual because it was a feast day and the locals were at leisure as well as the tourists, Sophie went up to the *torre*. Sacha was on duty at the camp, and Piet and Margriet had gone to see friends at Málaga, and would be away overnight.

When she had swum for a while, Sophie sunbathed until she was dry. Then she arranged a luxurious mound of cushions at one end of the canopied swing couch, and reclined in the shade of the awning to read *The Legend of the Two Discreet Statues* in her birthday book.

She was turning a page when, out of the corner of her eye, she glimpsed a movement at the far end of the pool. The next moment there was a splash. As the ripples cleared, she saw a long brown shape approaching under the water. Her eyes widened. Her heart gave a queer little jolt. But when Carlos swung himself out of the water, she showed no sign of the turmoil going on inside her.

"Good afternoon. I'm afraid the caretaker forgot to warn us you were coming," she said, in response to his, "Hello, Sophie. How are you?"

"There was no need for her to warn you. I am here alone this time, and you're welcome to use the pool as often as you would if the tower were closed."

She watched him stroll away to pick up the towel he had dropped when he entered the pool. It was the first time she had seen him undressed, and she was faintly surprised by

78

the strength of his tall, tanned figure. What did he do to look like that? It took more than spasmodic squash or weekly visits to an expensive gymnasium to maintain so patent a degree of fitness.

As he rough-towelled his head, and disappeared inside the tower, she debated making a swift getaway. But she had a feeling that the best way to cope with his unexpected return was to try to maintain an attitude of polite indifference.

Before she had made up her mind, he reappeared, wearing shorts, and carrying a vacuum jug in one hand and two tall glasses in the other.

Sophie swung her legs to the ground, and hurriedly placed her beach bag, sun hat and camera in the centre of the couch in the hope of preventing Carlos from sitting too close to her. She had brought the camera with the intention of taking some snaps of the courtyard and tower to send home. Her grandfather had become deeply interested in the Moorish rulers of Spain, and much of their correspondence was concerned with his researches and her reports of the Moorish ruins in the area.

If Carlos noticed the rearrangement of her belongings, and guessed the reason for it, he gave no sign.

"How are things going at the camp?" he enquired, sitting at the far end of the couch.

"We're packed out. Some of the campers didn't intend to come as far south as this, but there wasn't room for them in the Costa Blanca camps. Most of our present campers are spending the whole of their holiday here, but we've had some who were rushing through on the way to Morocco. I can't see the point of an overland trip to North Africa for people with only two or three weeks' holiday. As soon as they arrive, they have to turn round and head for home, with nothing to remember in the winter but mile after mile of main road."

"Mm, it does seem mad," he agreed. "A package flight to Morocco would be no more expensive, and far less exhausting. But no doubt there are some people who feel a sense of achievement merely because they have been a long way in a short time. In the 1980s, probably the standard holiday will be a month, and Andy Capp and his long-suffering wife will be caravanning to India and back."

He handed her a glass of chilled orange juice. As he did so, he noticed her book. "What are you reading?"

"A collection of stories about the Alhambra."

Carlos picked up the volume, and Sophie stifled the impulse to beg him to handle it gently. She knew from experience that even well-educated, mannerly people could not always – very seldom! – be trusted to treat old, rare books with the care they would give to a piece of antique porcelain. To her surprise, Carlos inspected the book in the unmistakable manner of a connoisseur. After a few minutes, he said, "Where did you pick this up?"

"It was given to me by someone who knew I was hoping to visit the Alhambra."

He laid the book on the squabs. "Excuse me a moment."

Watching him walk across the court, Sophie wondered why it had never occurred to her to consider that he might be a fellow collector. The fact that their first encounter had taken place in a second-hand bookshop had not seemed significant. Many people, other than collectors, visited shops like Bramfield's. Also, she had always associated book collecting with men of her grandfather's stamp; men who, even in youth, had inclined to intellectual rather than physical pleasures.

From the moment, more than four years ago, when she had cannoned into Carlos, and felt his strong hands on her shoulders, she had thought of him as a man of action. In Barcelona, his car, and even his choice of restaurant, had confirmed that first impression. Only a few minutes ago she had been struck by the toughness of his physique. Now, for the first time, she began to wonder if he was also a man for whom one of the pleasures of life was an evening of solitude among his books.

He came back carrying a large book which he put on her lap. "Same stories, differently packaged."

Sophie picked it up. The format was Large Imperial Octavo, uncomfortably heavy to hold in the hand. It was bound in full straight-grain morocco with raised bands on the lavishly tooled spine, and a crimson lettering piece. It had gilt edges, marbled endpapers, everything to impress the novice collector or someone who merely wanted a handsome shelf-filler. She liked the frontispiece, an engraving of a downcast maiden with a mandoline, but the title page showed that it was Volume IV of a collected edition of Irving's works published sixty years after her copy.

"Is this yours?" she asked.

"No. I don't know how it came here. Most of the books in the *sala* are there for ornamental purposes. They probably came from the houses of old uncles and aunts when they died. Most of them are Spanish, but there is a sprinkling of other languages. Would you consider swopping your copy for that one?"

"But if this book belongs to the Marqués, would he approve of your exchanging it for one which doesn't look as nice?" she asked.

"Hilario won't mind. I'll find him something suitable to replace it."

"You mean you want my copy for yourself? Why?"

Carlos was holding her copy in one well-shaped brown hand. He did not reply for a moment, and she found herself awaiting his answer with a good deal of tension.

He said, "This is an early edition which is of little interest to the average reader. But to someone who appreciates books as objects, as well as for their contents, your copy is the more desirable of the two. I'm sure you don't ill-treat any books, but one which is as old as this one deserves more than ordinary care."

"Is it valuable?"

"I can't tell you its market price. I know very little about Irving, beyond having read most of these stories, and his *Rip Van Winkle*, of course. This book isn't my field of interest. But I would make some effort to save any col-lectable book from the hazards of a summer on the Costa del Sol," he added dryly.

"Well, as it was a birthday present, I wouldn't sell it or swop it. But you needn't worry; it won't be left in the sun, or shoved in a bag with damp bathing things. My —" She broke off as the door in the wall opened, and Sacha entered the *patio*.

"Margriet has been on the telephone, Sophie. They have been in a road accident. Piet is in hospital in Málaga. They don't know yet how badly he is injured, but it is certain that he won't be coming back tomorrow."

"Oh, lord! Poor Margriet. Is she hurt?"

"No, fortunately she was shocked only."

Sophie realised the two men had not met, and she intro-duced them, wondering if Carlos would raise his eyebrows at the long necklace of beads and shells which Sacha was wearing with his Bermudas.

But evidently Carlos was too concerned by the bad news to pay any attention to the bearer's appearance. "Is Mar-griet at the hospital now? Did she say where you could con-tact her?" he asked.

Sacha shook his head. "No, only that she would tele-pone as soon as she had any more information. She is not alone. Their friends are with her."

"She and Piet had gone to spend the night with another Dutch couple who are living near Málaga," added Sophie.

"I'll go over, and see if I can help," said Carlos.

As he turned away, she said, "Don't forget your book," and handed it to him. He had left hers on the couch when he stood up to shake hands with Sacha.

"If Margriet should telephone again, tell her I'm on my way over," he said.

Walking down the hill with Sacha, Sophie said, "By the way, Carlos Walsingham is the owner of the camp. In that respect, it's lucky he happens to be here. He will know how to find replacements if Piet is laid low for some weeks. Presumably it wasn't a very bad accident if Margriet is unhurt?"

"I don't know," replied Sacha sombrely. "Usually it is the passenger who is most hurt. Perhaps Piet *was* the passenger. Margriet drives the car sometimes, doesn't she?"

"Yes, but she wasn't driving when they set out this morning. They may have stopped for coffee, and then changed places, of course."

About a quarter past ten, when most of the tents and caravans were in darkness, although the night was still young for the Spanish weekenders in the apartments, Sophie was in her caravan when there was a light knock on the Dutch door. When she opened the upper half, she found Carlos standing outside.

"Ah, you're still dressed. Good. The bar doesn't close for ten minutes. Come and have a coffee, and I'll tell you what has happened," he said. "Do you know where Sacha will be at this time of night?"

"In the bar, I expect. We only closed the kiosk a few minutes ago."

But Sacha was not in the open-air bar, and when Sophie suggested going to see if he was in the caravan, Carlos said,

"No, it doesn't matter. He can hear about it in the morning. What will you have? Coffee? Brandy?"

"Coffee, please." She climbed on to one of the tall stools along the counter. Apart from an elderly German couple, they had the place to themselves.

"Piet will be out of action for some weeks," said Carlos. "He has a broken arm, several broken ribs and his face and legs are badly cut. The car is a write-off. It's astonishing that Margriet wasn't hurt, but naturally she is very shaken up. The driver of the other car was killed, and for a time she thought Piet was dead too. Luckily her friend is a calm, sensible sort of woman, and she's going to stay with Margriet in a hotel close to the hospital."

"Have you any idea how it happened?"

"From what Margriet says, it seems that the other car burst a tyre at high speed and went out of control. Piet saw it coming at him, and managed to avert a head-on smash, but he couldn't avoid a partial collision. There'll be an enquiry, but I know an excellent lawyer in Málaga who will steer them through the proceedings."

He drank some of the brandy he had ordered for himself. He looked tired, thought Sophie. Perhaps he had motored a long way in the early part of the day, and the unforeseen drive to Málaga and back had depleted even his abundant vitality.

"Have you had any supper?" she asked.

"Not yet."

"Will there be food at the *torre* if the caretaker wasn't expecting you?"

"I bought eggs and a *chorizo* before I left Málaga. If the larder is bare, I can knock up an omelette," he answered. A slight smile touched his mouth. "But it's kind of you to be concerned for my welfare."

She lowered her gaze to her coffee cup. In her anxiety

84

about the Veenvelds, she had given little thought to the effect of his return on her own peace of mind.

She said coolly, "Will it be difficult to find temporary replacements for the Veenvelds? Sacha and I can hold the fort for a time, but not for several weeks."

"It won't be difficult to replace Piet. I shall take over his responsibilities myself. Whether a substitute for Margriet will be needed remains to be seen."

"You?" she exclaimed, startled. "Oh, but surely –"

"Surely what?" he prompted her, after a moment or two.

"Surely you have more important things to do than help out here? I thought you owned several hotels and motels and other businesses."

"I do, but it's in the low season, when alterations and improvements are made, that they need my attention. At this time of year they are in the hands of their managers. Therefore, as it was my intention to spend the next four weeks at the *torre* anyway, I may as well combine my holiday with a first-hand study of the camping aspect of *turismo*."

"I see," she said, filled with unease.

The German couple had gone, and the barman was tidying up, preparatory to closing. She finished her coffee, and slid off the stool.

"Thank you for telling me the latest news. It's a relief to know that Piet won't be permanently disabled."

Carlos stood up. "Goodnight, Sophie."

"Goodnight."

As she made her way back to her caravan, exchanging quiet goodnights in several languages with campers strolling to and from the shower-house, her thoughts were in as much of a whirl as on the night he had escorted her down the hill.

Why had he decided to spend a month at the *torre*? She felt sure it had not been his intention at the time of his previous visit. Could it be that her parting shot on that occasion had chafed his masculine vanity to the point of making him determined to make her eat her words? The prospect of having to hold out against a persistent and practised campaign to bring her to heel made Sophie quail. Had he been an elderly lecher who gave her the creeps merely by looking at her, she would have felt much less perturbation. Resistance based on genuine repugnance was invincible. But to resist a man who was wildly attractive was another matter. Were her principles stronger than her senses? Could her head overrule her heart?

The more she thought about it, the more she was convinced that no man in Carlos's position would choose to holiday on the Costa del Sol in midsummer unless he had some special reason for putting up with crowds when he could be relaxing in a resort exclusive to the rich. True, the *torre* was more luxurious than the most de luxe hotel, and the private swimming pool made it unnecessary for him to mingle with the masses on the beach. But as far as she knew the nearest sophisticated night life was in Málaga, or perhaps in Granada. Almuñecar catered for the middle-income family man of all nations, and the international blue jeans set. Not the jet set.

She slept badly, and at half past five the next morning she was on her way to the beach. The only other person about was an English boy of about twelve who was fishing from the rocks below the *torre*. Otherwise the cove was as peaceful as it must have been all summer long before the tourist boom.

Sophie had no patience with the selfish outlook sometimes expressed by older people that *turismo* was spoiling the Spanish seaboard. It seemed to her a splendid thing that now people who spent most of the year in factories and shops and offices in the grey northern cities could afford to come south to the sun. It was better for the local population, too. A thousand package tourists brought more prosperity than a handful of villa-owners.

Nevertheless she loved the first hours of the day when the brown hills were veiled by a haze, and the sea had a mother-of-pearl sheen. When the sun rose it did not give the harsh glare of noon, but shed a soft golden light which left parts of the landscape in purple shadow. At this hour of the morning there were no transistors playing, no resonant Spanish voices shouting down from upper balconies to people passing below, no hum of traffic from the coast road. The day began slowly and gently, and merely to stand waist-deep in the warm, calm sea was infinitely refreshing.

She had been swimming for about twenty minutes when she saw with dismay, and a treacherous undercurrent of excitement, that the boy had an onlooker. Carlos, in boxer shorts, with a towel slung over his shoulder, was chatting to him. As she trod water, watching them, he glanced towards her and raised a hand in recognition. Then he picked his way round the rocks to a diving place well away from the boy's line.

She had guessed he would dive and swim with the ease of someone to whom water was a familiar element, not with the unaccustomed air of many of the holidaymakers. When she saw him surface and turn in her direction, powered by a strong but leisurely crawl, she had an impulse to make for the shore as fast as possible. She knew from playful experiences with Guy on the Ile d'Oleron that it was impossible to resist being kissed when one was out of one's depth in the sea. However it was already too late to sprint for the beach. If he chose, he could intercept her easily.

To her relief, Carlos stopped swimming before he

reached her. At a distance of two or three metres, he began to tread water. "Good morning."

"Good morning."

"You shouldn't swim alone. You might get cramp."

"I wasn't alone. The boy was there when I arrived."

"He may not swim."

"Boys who like fishing usually can." She rolled over and began to swim towards one of several powerboats which were anchored a hundred yards offshore.

Carlos followed her until, nearing the blue and white launch, he put on a burst of speed and passed her. By the time she had reached the shadow of the hull, he had hauled himself inboard and was holding out a helping hand to her.

She shook her head. "I must go back now. I like to do my washing when the laundry room is empty."

She was about a third of the way to the beach when she heard him dive from the boat. They waded out of the sea side by side.

"Do you find the amenities at the camp satisfactory? Have you any criticisms?" he asked.

"No, I think it's an excellent camp. There was a spot of bother soon after I arrived. In the absence of any power points in the women's half of the shower-house, a French girl marched into the men's section to plug in her hair-dryer. She annoyed several men who were in there at the time, but Piet smoothed them down, and had some more power points installed. I suppose whoever planned the shower-house didn't realise that women also use electric razors; not to mention dryers and heated rollers."

"It's a point to bear in mind with future camps. From what I have seen, and been told, the Germans lead the field in providing the best amenities, and maintaining the highest standard of hygiene. But of course many things which make cool climate camping more enjoyable – for example, metered hot showers – are superfluous here."

He was still talking about camping when they reached the door in the wall. "Can I offer you some coffee?" he said. "Real coffee, not the instant variety."

"No, thank you, Carlos. 'Dios" – using the Spanish equivalent of 'Bye.

She turned and walked on a few paces.

"Sophie."

She halted. "Yes?"

"I think I should make something clear to you. If you are nervous that I may take advantage of our working relationship at the camp to pursue my dishonourable intentions, you have no need to worry. As long as I am in charge here, you are quite safe." A glimmer of amusement lit his eyes. "Unless you yourself indicate that virtue is no longer its own reward. See you later. 'Dios." This time it was he who turned away.

A week later, Sophie drove along the coast to Málaga to see Margriet and Piet. For some way beyond Almuñecar the road wound up and down and in and out of the dry gullies interspersing the high rose-red cliffs. As she rounded one of the bends, she came upon a grinning gypsy boy who waved *esparto* baskets enticingly at her. Sophie returned his grin, but shook her head at the baskets. Further on she saw his family. They were helping a donkey to pull their laden waggon up a hill. They grinned and waved. As she passed them, she glimpsed in the rear view mirror the dark-skinned face and fine teeth of one of the older sons. His bold, merry expression reminded her of the way Carlos had looked at her across the crowded room at Mrs. Hackenbacker's party in Barcelona.

After Nerja, the coastline flattened and all the way along, where once there had been only fishing villages, fourteen-storey white buildings were mushrooming on both sides of the road.

She found Margriet installed in a suite in an expensive hotel.

"This is Carlos's doing, and he insists on paying the bill," said the Dutch girl, showing her visitor the air-conditioned bedroom and opulent bathroom.

"He's a wealthy man. It won't break him."

"He is generous with more than his money," Margriet said reprovingly. "He came immediately, and he was a great comfort because, being half Spanish, he knows the customs of the country, and where to find a good lawyer – everything of that kind. Whatever you may think of him, Sophie, I know he has a warm heart and would always help anyone in trouble. There is another thing about him; most men do not like women to cry. I was very upset all day after the accident. I could not stop crying, but Carlos was not embarrassed. He held my hand and talked quietly to me, and was so nice I can't tell you."

They returned to the fan-cooled sitting-room. She asked, "What is it like with him in charge at the camp? Piet was astonished when he heard about it."

"He spends a lot of time chatting to the campers. Manolo had his head bitten off because a woman complained that the melons in the camp shop were twice the price of melons in the *mercado* at Almuñecar, and also that some rusks she had bought at the shop were damp instead of crisp."

"But you and Sacha have not had your heads bitten off?"

"Not yet. Oddly enough, Carlos doesn't seem to share Mike's contempt for Sacha. They sometimes play chess together when the camp is quiet in the afternoon."

"Carlos has not asked you to dine with him at the *torre*?"

"No." Sophie changed the subject. "How is Piet? Is he making good progress?"

After lunch they visited Piet who did his best to appear cheerful, but who was obviously suffering considerable discomfort from his fractures and cuts and general bruising. In the evening the two girls dined at one of the city's noted fish restaurants where they sampled Malagueña soup and grilled red mullet.

Sophie spent the night in the other twin divan in Margriet's cool bedroom. Next morning she went, alone, to see the seventeenth-century choir stalls in the Cathedral which Grandplum had urged her to visit if she had the opportunity.

"During the Civil War", he had written in the letter which she had with her, and re-read before setting out, "the Republicans housed poor families in the side chapels. These people used the altars to cook on, and religious effigies for fuel. Why Pedro de Mena's carvings were not destroyed is a mystery, but they sound worth seeing. How I wish I were twenty years younger, and could see them for myself!"

It was late afternoon when she returned to the familiar territory between Almuñecar and Torre del Moro. Half way between the town and the camp she saw Carlos's car parked under a tree at the roadside. Behind it was a sporty scarlet Lancia whose driver, a glamorous creature in a halter-necked white sun top and navy and white Oxford bags, was chatting animatedly to Carlos while he changed a wheel for her.

To Sophie's subsequent chagrin, she was so fascinated by this spectacle that she forgot to look in her windscreen mirror before she decelerated, thereby causing the driver of a following car to brake, hoot, swerve round her and yell out of the window as he did so.

Inevitably this caused both Carlos and the girl to turn and stare. Her face flaming, Sophie drove on.

To her surprise, about twenty minutes later Carlos strolled up to the kiosk where she had stopped to tell Sacha the news from Málaga. Even more to her surprise, he said nothing about the incident on the road, but merely asked her how Piet was.

Later, taking a shower, she found the fact that he had not mocked her oddly dispiriting.

The following afternoon when she was on duty at the kiosk while Sacha had some time off, she noticed something lying on one of the shelves beneath the counter which, when she realised what it was, gave her a start of surprise and pleasure. It was the summer number of *The Book Collector*, a scholarly quarterly to which Mr. Lingwood subscribed and in which his granddaughter could generally find a good deal to interest her.

She was deep in an article on British Bindings when Carlos said, "Wouldn't you find this more entertaining?" He held up a dog-eared paperback copy of a current best-seller. "Someone dropped it on the path to the beach." He added the title to the list of 'things found' on the notice-board.

"This is yours, presumably?" said Sophie, handing him *The Book Collector*.

"Yes. Very dry stuff, except to a few *aficionados*."

Her vexation at not being able to finish the article, and at his assumption that she could not find such a periodical interesting, made her say in a carefully flat voice, "I would need a dictionary to explain all those long words."

His grey eyes narrowed. "Sarcasm, Sophie? Is it possible that you are an *aficionada*?"

She said evasively, "My grandfather is a book collector. I know a little about it."

"Was it he who gave you Irving's *Alhambra*?"

"Yes."

"And you knew the relative values of your copy and the copy I offered you?"

"Yes, I did."

"It's as well I didn't try to make out that your copy was worthless," he said dryly.

"I thought you were remarkably scrupulous. Collectors sometimes aren't. Perhaps you wouldn't have been if I'd had something you wanted very badly. What is your field?"

Before he could answer, a Dormobile drew up and the driver leaned out to ask if they had a vacant space. For fifteen minutes Sophie was busy attending to the newcomers, and during that time she made up her mind to avoid any further conversation about book collecting. But it seemed a particularly cruel irony of fate that Carlos should turn out to be a bibliophile. If only he had been a man of ordinary means, with a different attitude to women, how well they could have got on, she thought wistfully. What a happy summer this would have been if Carlos had been in Sacha's shoes, and Sacha the occupant of the *torre*.

"Did you go to see the caves at Nerja on your way to Málaga last week?" asked Mike, when he and Sophie were chatting in the central avenue of the camp one morning.

"No, I didn't. I don't know that caves appeal to me very much."

"You ought not to miss the ones at Nerja. Even General Franco has been to them."

"Really? Well, I can't go over this afternoon. My car is being serviced. I'll go next week perhaps."

"I'm going to Nerja this afternoon. Why don't you come with me? You can look round the caves while I'm attending to my business there."

Sophie hesitated. She was not sure that she wanted to spend a couple of hours in Mike's company. There was something slightly cranky about him. He had several bees in his bonnet, and although she sensed that he was a lonely person who needed someone to listen to him, he was also a bigoted man with prejudices she did not share. If he started one of his diatribes while they were chatting at the beach bar, it was not too difficult to escape. But once in his car she would be stuck.

"It's very kind of you, Mike, but –"

"You're welcome. I'll be glad of your company. I'll pick you up at the main gate at four o'clock." And before she could extricate herself, he had gone on his way.

Later in the morning she was strolling round the camp to check that all the bins had been emptied, and that no one was playing a transistor radio or otherwise upsetting their neighbours, when Carlos fell into step with her.

"Sophie, I think it would be better if you wore a dress while you're on duty," he said briskly.

"Why, yes . . . if you wish," she answered, in surprise. "But Margriet always wears a swimsuit. So does everyone" – with a gesture at all the campers in sight.

"They are here to enjoy themselves. Most of them are middle-aged women, and I don't think it heightens their enjoyment to see their husbands admiring your charms."

Considering that she never bought very skimpy bikinis because they tended to come adrift if worn for the energetic diving and swimming which she enjoyed, Sophie felt it was rather unfair to instruct her to wear cotton frocks. There were girls in the camp whose bikinis were far more revealing than her coral, yellow and cornflower stretch-terry two-pieces.

"Are you going to make Sacha wear a shirt in case it annoys the middle-aged men to see their wives admiring *his* charms?" she asked lightly.

To her astonishment, Carlos halted and faced her. He

94

said in a quiet, steel-cold voice, "You already have my word that I won't overstep the bounds of our present working relationship. Do I need to remind *you* that it is a working relationship, and that even though I may express my wishes in the form of requests rather than orders, I don't expect them to be questioned?"

"I – I'm sorry," she stammered, taken aback by the unprecedented severity of his manner. "Naturally I'll obey your wishes. I'll go and change now."

"Going into town?" asked Sacha when, soon after this, he met her wearing white pants and a navy check sleeveless shirt.

"Carlos has told me not to wear a bathing suit in camp."

"Don't frown about it. It's a compliment. You must take his mind off his work," remarked Sacha, with a grin.

"Not his mind. He thinks I appeal to ageing husbands. Although why I should be a distraction when there are people like that about . . ." She finished the sentence with a nod at a passing French girl in a minimal brown wet-look bikini with a gilt chain round her undulating hips, and platform-soled sandals.

"I don't think she would interest Carlos. If one can compare women with wine, *mademoiselle* is what in England you call 'plonk'. You, English miss, are a wine of the *grand premier cru*."

"Oh, Sacha, what a splendid piece of flattery," she said, laughing. "What with being taken to task by Carlos this morning, and having to go to Nerja with Mike this afternoon, I was feeling decidedly low. You've cheered me up beautifully."

"Why are you going to Nerja with Mike?"

She explained. To her dismay he grimaced, and then gave a shrug. "I guess you won't have too much trouble with him. You're a tall, strong girl, and he's not much of a man."

"I'm not expecting *any* trouble of that kind. Mike never ogles me."

"Not when you might see him doing it. But when you aren't looking at him –" He pantomimed exaggerated lust.

Sophie grinned, reasured that he was only teasing her. For a moment she had thought he was serious.

"Who is looking after the bar, Mike? Or have you closed it?" she asked, as they set out for Nerja.

"I pay a local boy to mind it sometimes. He only speaks Spanish, but people can point to what they want. Ha! I never thought five years ago I'd be running a beach bar in Spain."

"What were you doing at that time?"

The question was the cue to a monologue which lasted until he drove into the car-park by the caves. Almost from his opening boast that he had been a stockbroker with a large flat in Cadogan Square and a country house in the Cotswolds, Sophie knew that the story of his past was a fabrication. He was such a fluent, detailed liar that she might have enjoyed his inventions but for the fact that he was also a hair-raising driver.

By the time he switched off the motor, she had had enough tension for one day. "Look, I'm not sure how long I'll be, and I don't want to keep you hanging about. I'll catch a bus back to camp, Mike. They seem to run fairly frequently, and it will be a chance to talk to some Andalusians."

"No, no. I can't allow that. It's too slow, and too hot, going by bus. I'll come back for you in an hour. I don't mind waiting," he insisted.

The Caves of Nerja were impressive. From a narrow entrance, then a small museum of prehistoric tools and bones, a staircase descended into the Sala de Cataclismo, a chamber as vast and awesome as a cathedral. Concealed coloured lighting gave some idea of the beauty of the place when it was first discovered, before the lights of the twentieth century had quenched for ever the brief, magic, jewel-bright glitter and shimmer of rocks lost in darkness, unseen by man, for three thousand years.

By the time she emerged into the sunlit warmth of the upper air, Sophie had forgotten her dread of the homeward drive. With ten minutes to spare before Mike came for her, she chose some postcards to send home, and enjoyed an iced *limonada* on a terrace with a panoramic view.

Several hours later, as she was wandering forlornly round Nerja, killing time because the coastal bus service was not as frequent as she had thought, a white car drew up alongside her.

"Can I run you home?" Carlos asked.

"What are you doing in Nerja?" she asked cautiously, when she was seated beside him, and the car was in motion.

"Looking for you. When your cavalier returned without you, Sacha became concerned. As he hasn't a car, he prevailed on me to come to your resue. I must say that, for a girl of your age, with your looks, you seem extraordinarily bad at recognising the predatory male and avoiding embarrassing situations."

Sophie said nothing. Lapped in the comfort of his car, and the curious security of his presence, she found herself foolishly close to tears.

"When did you last have some food?"

"At lunch time, but I'm not hungry."

"You may not be. I am. We'll eat at El Cortijo Blanco."

When she came out of the *Señoras* in the small, converted farmhouse restaurant a kilometre off the main road, having combed her hair and put on lipstick, Carlos was drinking sherry with a look of frowning abstraction. He rose to his feet as she joined him and, meeting his unsmiling

97

gaze, she wondered if she was to be interrogated as well as fed.

He had ordered *arroz en costra*, rice and chicken in a blanket of crisp batter, with salad and a potent red wine. She began to feel less downcast, especially as he did not harry her with questions.

"What did you think of the caves?" he asked. And, when that topic was exhausted, "Tell me about your grandfather and his books."

She told him, but carefully avoiding any remark which would reveal her personal interest in the subject. Once or twice when she looked up from the food on her plate, she found him studying her face with a peculiarly keen scrutiny which made her wonder if talking about books had caused something to click in his memory. Now, realising how foolish it had been of her ever to hope that he would remember her, the last thing she wanted was to be recognised as the schoolgirl he had kissed years ago.

It was for this reason that, when he asked, "Where does your grandfather live?", instead of telling the truth, she named a town thirty miles from the resort in which she had grown up.

It was dark when they passed through Almuñecar. The *torre* being accessible only on foot, Carlos kept his car in a shaded space behind the block of *apartamientos*.

As they walked from there to the camp, Sophie said, "Thank you very much for bringing me back, and for dinner. I don't know what you think happened, but –"

"Spare me an explanation," he cut in sardonically. "But as it isn't the first time you've landed in this type of contretemps, I think you should try to be a little less naïve in future. Goodnight, Sophie." And with a nod of dismissal, he turned aside to speak to a grizzled old Spaniard with whom he was evidently acquainted.

Sacha was talking to a camper when she approached the kiosk, so she turned round and went to her caravan, deciding to have an early night.

She was boiling an egg for breakfast on the portable stove which was part of the caravan's equipment when Sacha paused on his way back from the shower-house the next morning.

"I was right about Mike and you, eh?" he said. "What did Carlos say when he found you? Or had he cooled down by that time?"

"What do you mean — 'cooled down'?" she asked.

"He was not pleased when I told him you had gone to Nerja with Mike. But when Mike came back without you — pow!"

"He said *you* had persuaded him to come for me."

Sacha looked blank. "I didn't say anything. He didn't ask my opinion. He asked Mike why you were not with him, and Mike looked embarrassed and said he didn't see what it had to do with Carlos, but you had decided to come back by bus. So then Carlos said there was nothing special to see in Nerja, apart from the *cuevas*, and he would be held responsible if anything bad had happened to you. So Mike had better tell him the truth — inmediamente!"

"But that's nonsense. Why should he be held responsible? And what could possibly happen to me in a harmless little town like Nerja?"

"Maybe he thought you would try to hitch-hike back. I know he thinks it is dangerous for girls to travel that way. He is half Spanish, and in Spain unmarried girls are still more protected than in other countries."

"Spanish girls may be protected, but I'm sure Carlos doesn't feel the smallest obligation to protect foreign girls," replied Sophie, in a wry tone. "What happened then?"

"Then Mike admitted there had been a disagreement between you, and Carlos told him to pack his bags and get to hell out of it."

"Out of the camp, d'you mean?"

"Out of the camp, out of the bar, out of the province," said Sacha dramatically.

"You mean Carlos owns the beach bar, and he *sacked* Mike?"

He nodded. "But I think there were other reas—" he began.

But Sophie was no longer listening. "Could you eat this boiled egg? I'm going up to the *torre* to beg an audience with the all-powerful Mr. Walsingham," she said, with a sparkle in her eyes.

For once the tranquil beauty of the leafy courtyard failed to make her pause and catch her breath when she pushed open the door in the wall. This morning she marched resolutely round the edge of the pool, and tugged at the chain which rang an ancient bell, producing a deep, gong-like clangour which must have roused any campers who were still asleep.

As she waited for a response to this summons, it occurred to her that Carlos might not yet be up. But even if he were still in bed, the bell must rouse him eventually, and there was no time to be lost if Mike was to be reinstated.

In fact it was not more than a minute or two before the great iron-studded door swung inwards, and Carlos raised an interrogative eyebrow at the sight of his early caller. He was wearing a thin navy silk dressing gown over pyjama trousers of navy and white check Dacron (judging by his bare chest, he dispensed with the jacket), but he had shaved, and his hair was brushed.

"I would like to talk to you," Sophie announced, in a firm tone.

"By all means. Come in. No, on second thoughts perhaps it would be more *decoroso* if I came out. I won't keep you long."

Waiting for him to reappear, she paced round the pool, wishing she had not allowed him to brush aside her attempted explanation the night before. But even if she had realised Mike was one of his concessionaires, it would never have occurred to her that Carlos would take such drastic action.

When he joined her, he had changed into a shirt and shorts, and was carrying a breakfast tray on which, she noticed, there were two cups.

"Coffee?" he asked, placing the tray on a white table.

"No, thank you. I've already had mine."

He gave her an enigmatic look. "Do sit down, Sophie. If you don't, I can't, and I prefer to have breakfast sitting down. Would you care for some fruit?" – indicating five or six downy peaches nestling in a napkin-lined basket.

She shook her head impatiently. "You seem very concerned with being *decoroso* all of a sudden."

He gave a slight shrug. "When in Spain . . ."

"You were in Spain at the Miramar," she reminded him.

Carlos began to peel a peach. "A hotel is a no man's land where people behave according to their lights. Here I am, in effect, my cousin's guest, and you are a young and rather foolish virgin – a fact of which I was not aware at the Miramar!"

"But not so young or so foolish as to let you seduce me," she retorted. "Or to be unable to cope with someone like Mike. Sacha says you have dismissed him. Doesn't that make you feel a hypocrite?"

"Not in the least," he said calmly.

"Well, it should," she told him indignantly. "To sack a man because you suspect him of attempting the very same thing you once tried yourself seems to me the acme of

101

hypocrisy."

"I don't recall that I ever left a girl stranded twenty-five miles from home, possibly without any alternative transport, and possibly without any money."

"Mike didn't leave me stranded. I left him – but not for the same reason that I left the Miramar," she added accusingly.

"Anyone hearing your denunciatory references to the Miramar would think you had had to defend your virtue by force," Carlos answered dryly. "It wasn't quite such a narrow escape, if you remember."

"I'm not likely to forget it! You may not have stranded me, but you forced me to drive far further than twenty-five miles to find somewhere else to spend the night."

"On the contrary, I didn't force you to leave, and I wouldn't have forced unwelcome attentions on you had you stayed. You panicked, as girls of your sort are apt to do in those circumstances."

"I suppose you think girls of my sort are an amusing anachronism?" she said, in a low voice.

"By no means. In Spain the majority of unmarried girls are chaste. The permissive society has a very limited influence here. It's because I was brought up to respect such girls that I was concerned for your welfare yesterday." He paused, and once again he looked at her with the expression she could not interpret. "Considering that, north of the Pyrenees, the pressures are mostly in the other direction, and you are anything but unattractive, you must have considerable strength of character to have stuck to your unfashionable principles."

"It doesn't call for great powers of resistance to refuse stale buns if, at the end of the day, one is going to a banquet," said Sophie.

"I've been called many things, but never a stale bun,"

Carlos remarked, with a poker face.

Then the skin at the top of his high *morisco* cheekbones started to crinkle, and she knew he was going to laugh. It was hard to hold aloof when he laughed. Against her will she felt her mouth wanting to curve in response. It had been his look of humour, of being quick to enjoy life's absurdities, which had appealed to her strongly in Barcelona. Now, although she knew he was laughing at her, the sight and sound of his amusement made her ache to be on easy terms with him. But they were not, and they never could be, so she pulled her mouth down, and said earnestly, "Please, Carlos, you can't sack Mike for doing nothing. I didn't want to come home with him chiefly because he's such an abominable driver. I admit I was slightly uneasy when he took me to somebody's empty villa, and said we could picnic on the veranda. But probably, if I'd stayed, he would only have told more tall stories. I think he's a rather pathetic misfit. I'm sure he wouldn't have been . . . threatening."

The amusement had died out of his eyes. "You are wasting your breath, my girl. I don't know where he has gone, and if I did it would make no difference."

He saw her shoulders sag, and made an exasperated sound. "Oh, don't be such a goose, Sophie. Do you seriously think I would have sent him packing for that reason alone? The man had been a nuisance for some time. His manner was generally morose, his standard of hygiene was low, and I had had several reports of his drinking too much and behaving badly in Almuñecar. I suspect that Piet wanted to get rid of him but shirked taking action. I had no such compunction. Misfits and drop-outs do considerable harm to the reputation of their countries. Perhaps, having a foot in two camps, I'm more aware of that fact than most people."

For a moment or two she said nothing. Then, slowly, she

rose to her feet. "I see. In that case I'm sorry I bothered you unnecessarily. I'll let you get on with your breakfast in peace." She turned away.

He called her back, his expression no longer as severe as when he was speaking of Mike. "That banquet you were talking about – How long are you prepared to wait?"

"Perhaps all my life," she said quietly. "I suppose that seems silly to you."

He shrugged. "Not silly. Merely very young. Have you read much of Robert Louis Stevenson?"

"Only *Treasure Island* and *Doctor Jekyll and Mr. Hyde.*"

"There's a book of his called *Travels with a Donkey* which summed up my ideas on the subject when I was your age. How old are you? Nineteen? Twenty?"

"I'm twenty-one. How old are you?"

His mouth quirked. "Too old to believe in Stevenson's formula for the good life, or to hope for perfection in one woman."

"I don't hope for perfection, only –" She stopped. "I must go. Sacha will be waiting for me."

Sacha, when she joined him at the kiosk, said, "Did he listen to you?"

She shook her head. "I listened to him."

Later in the morning she happened to pass the caravan Mike had occupied when Rosario, one of the cleaners, was turning it out. She beckoned the English girl to come and look at the interior.

"Behold, *señorita* – would you believe that anyone but a pig could live in such dirt?" she exclaimed in the husky slurred Andaluz which at last Sophie was beginning to master.

Sophie was shocked and ashamed that an Englishman had perpetrated such squalor. Mike had seemed reasonably clean in his person, but his living quarters were disgusting.

The next time she went to Almuñecar, she looked for *Travels with a Donkey*. But most of the English paperbacks on sale were thrillers or 'the book of the film'. Although the proprietor of the town's bookshop could offer her several Spanish hardback novels by 'Carlos' Dickens, he had nothing by Robert Louis Stevenson.

She debated writing to Grandplum to ask him to send her the Penguin edition, but then she thought she would be sure to find a copy in Granada, which was a university city. She was deeply curious to know the formula for happiness which had appealed to Carlos in his salad days, but in which he no longer believed.

CHAPTER FOUR

BEFORE Piet and Margriet came back to Torre del Moro, Carlos found a Danish couple to take over the management of the beach bar, and he hired two more Dutch girls to augment the staff at the camp.

On the day following the Veenvelds' return, Sophie was able to embark on her overdue visit to Granada. She was accompanied by Sacha who also had a long weekend due to him, and who had asked her, in Carlos's hearing, if she would give him a lift in her car.

"I notice you raised no objection to my taking Sacha as a passenger," she had remarked to Carlos later on, when the other man was no longer present.

"On the contrary, you'll find him useful if you should need a wheel changed," he answered. "There's not much traffic on the road between Almuñecar and Granada. The road from Motril is the busiest route from the coast. On the 'back' road, you could wait a long time before help came."

"I wouldn't have to wait. I know how to change a wheel."

"I expect you do. I know how to sew on a button. But why spoil your hands unnecessarily? And there might be other contingencies you couldn't cope with."

"Is the back road a hair-raising one?"

"Not at all. I should say it's safer than the Motril road by virtue of the lack of traffic. You needn't worry about having to drive along unguarded precipices."

It was eight o'clock in the morning when Sophie and Sacha set out. On the outskirts of Almuñecar, instead of entering the town they took the turning by the mule trough which led to the *vega*, the fertile plain surrounding the dry river bed of the Rio Verde.

As they drove through the *vega*, towards the brown hills of the hinterland, Sacha pointed out groves of *chirimoyos*, a tree of South American origin which grew only in this part of Spain, and which bore a fruit in outward appearance like an artichoke.

"I hear they're delicious. But they're not exported, and this is not the season to eat them," he said regretfully.

"Where are you planning to stay in Granada?" Sophie asked him. Her own intention was to put up at a camp called Los Alamos, a few kilometres outside the city. It had been recommended to her by two young English doctors, honeymooning in a tent, who had been to Granada the week before and were now at Torre del Moro.

"I'll find somewhere," Sacha said vaguely.

By the time they had fixed a rendezvous for the return journey, the road had wound uphill to Otivar which Carlos had said was the last hamlet on the road. Above Otivar there were only a few isolated inns and farms.

Thinking of Carlos, and wondering if he would still be at the *torre* when she got back, took much of the edge off Sophie's enthusiasm for the trip. Now that the Veenvelds were back there was no reason for him to remain. But surely he would have mentioned his intention to leave? Surely he would have said goodbye to her?

Maybe not, she thought gloomily, steering the car round the first of a long succession of steep hairpin bends.

Vehicles climbing to Granada hugged the hillside. Vehicles descending to the coast drove on the open side of the road, but the edge was clearly defined by spaced blocks of granite which, seen from a distance, looked like the crenellations of an endless battlement.

The hills, which looked so barren from a distance, were

unexpectedly well wooded, and at intervals there were notices warning drivers to be alert for wild game. However the only animals they saw were some small black and chocolate brown goats, and a somnolent mule carrying an old man and a load of brushwood.

At first it seemed they would soon reach the summit of the climb. But each time they seemed to be approaching the top, a fold in the hills revealed further heights to be scaled. At last, when they had been droning steadily uphill for over an hour, the wild ochreous landscape of immense ravines and rocky bluffs gave place to an undulating route across a plateau of moorland.

Presently the moorland became partially cultivated, and by ten o'clock the city of Granada lay before them and, above it, the towering peaks of the Sierra Nevada, snow-capped even in the burning heat of midsummer.

The environs of the city were a hurly-burly of new and half-built high-rise *apartamientos*, office blocks and shops. When they had to stop at some temporary traffic lights, Sophie watched a labourer in cement-dusty jeans and a vivid tangerine safety helmet steering a barrow along a plank and singing, not the ubiquitous "pop" of northern Europe, but an impromptu outburst of *cante jondo*. *Flamenco* music had always appealed to her, but this was the first time she had heard it in its natural setting, sung in a powerful voice by a man who looked as if his ancestry was as mixed and mysterious as the origin of the harsh, throbbing notes which poured from his throat. Part gypsy, part Moor, perhaps part Phoenician, he sang with such an ancient melancholy that Sophie felt a shiver down her spine.

It took a gentle nudge from Sacha to make her notice that the traffic lights had changed, and this realisation was followed by the discovery that the engine was not idling but was dead.

About an hour later, when the car was in the nearest garage, and it was apparent that finding and repairing the cause of the trouble was likely to take some time, Sophie decided that in order not to spoil Sacha's weekend – he refused to leave her to cope with the situation alone – she would have to forget Los Alamos, and find somewhere to stay in the city.

Late the following afternoon she stepped gratefully into the shade of the vine which formed an airy green canopy over the side entrance to the church of San Jerónimo. To her surprise and pleasure the great church was empty. Of all the hundreds of tourists in Granada that day, it seemed that she alone was interested in the burial place of Fernando Gonzalo de Cordoba, the immortal Gran Capitán.

She had been in the church for a few minutes, and was sitting below the pink marble pulpit, enjoying the quiet and the coolness after the heat of the streets, when, to her astonishment, Carlos came in.

"You are 'doing' Granada very thoroughly," he said, as he sat down beside her. "Most people don't bother to come here."

"I wanted to see the statue of El Gran Capitán," she explained, glancing at the painted effigies of the great soldier and his wife at prayer on either side of the altar. "What brings you here?"

"Next week I'm going to stay with my cousins at their summer place in the mountains near Ronda. I came to Granada to buy a birthday present for Luisa. While I was in a shop near here, I saw you walk past. I followed because I thought it possible that you and Sacha might like to hear some good *flamenco* tonight. But perhaps you don't know where he is staying."

"Yes, I do. In half an hour I'm meeting him in the Plaza

del Carmen. I'm sure he'd like to hear *flamenco* as much as I should."

So her surmise had been correct. He was going away. She should have felt relief. Instead she felt a sharp pang of despair.

"In that case, I'll walk back with you," said Carlos. "Why are you interested in El Gran Capitán?"

"He was one of my heroes as a schoolgirl. His effigy is a little disappointing. I always thought of him as a tall man, and much darker in colouring."

"I should have thought his treatment of his wife would have alienated your affection for him."

"What do you mean? I never read that he was cruel to her."

"No, not cruel, but didn't you know that when Queen Isabella's tent caught fire and all her clothes went up in flames, he made his bride hand over her trousseau?"

"I expect he replaced it later on. Perhaps it was Isabella he loved. There are one or two hints that he might have done, and I'm sure she must have preferred him to her own tiresome husband, Ferdinand."

Carlos looked amused. "I fancy Isabella was like Elizabeth the First. They were queens first, and women second. Have you seen Isabella's tomb in the Chapel Royal?"

"Yes, yesterday; and early this morning I walked up the hill to the Alhambra." She glanced at her watch. "I think we ought to be going."

Outside it seemed hotter than ever. Carlos put his hand under her elbow to steer her across the street in front of the church. "Was it up to your expectations?"

"How can you ask? Those incredible honeycomb ceilings, and the maze of dim rooms with unexpected glimpses of the pools and gardens outside. But even though I went early, soon there were guided parties going round. To enjoy it to perfection one would have to be there alone." Or with a person one loved, she added mentally.

When they reached the Plaza del Carmen, five minutes early, Sacha was nowhere to be seen.

"Something cold to drink, or would you prefer an ice?" asked Carlos when, at his suggestion, they were seated in a pavement café outside the Club Taurino on the shady side of the busy square.

"A cold drink, please." She was conscious that the city had taken on a sparkle which it had not had for her an hour ago. It was not the Alhambra she would remember, but this bustling, undistinguished *plaza*, the sonorous voices of half a dozen old men in conversation behind them, and Carlos's brown hand resting on the edge of the table.

"Where do your cousins live in the winter?" she asked.

"In Seville which is uncomfortably hot in the summer. From the end of May to October, Luisa and the children spend most of their time at the *cortijo*, and Hilario joins them as often as he can. Here comes Sacha."

She had hoped Sacha might be late, and was surprised Carlos had recognised him so quickly as, since their arrival in Granada, the Frenchman had suddenly assumed a more conservative appearance.

When she had remarked on this alteration, Sacha had replied that clothes which were suitable for the beach were not appropriate for visiting museums and cathedrals, and although he had no religious beliefs himself, he thought it stupid to ignore the codes observed by older people.

Now, coming towards them, carrying a small parcel, he could pass for a Spanish boy on his way to work after the *siesta*. His short sleeved cotton-knit shirt was tucked inside tight but well-pressed trousers, and his shoes looked as if they had recently received the expert attention of one of the city's many boot-blacks.

111

"I passed a bookshop and found two of the books you wanted," he said to Sophie, after Carlos's presence had been explained to him.

She had been uneasily aware of the parcel for some minutes. When she had said to Sacha that, if he happened to come across a good bookshop during his perambulations about the city, she would be glad if he would note its whereabouts or even enquire about the books she wanted, it had never occurred to her that Carlos would suddenly appear on the scene.

"Thank you. How much do I owe you?"

"There is a bill in the bag." He opened the paper bag, extracting not only the bill but also the two paperbacks. One of them was Gautier's *Wanderings in Spain* which Sacha himself had recommended. The other was the book she most wanted to read but which, in present circumstances, she found as embarrassing as if it were a volume of erotica she had asked him to procure for her.

It was too much to hope that Carlos would pay no attention to the books, and to snatch them out of Sacha's hand and attempt to stuff them into her already full shoulder-bag might make matters worse.

Sure enough, as she opened her purse and found the pesetas to repay the Frenchman, Carlos reached across the table and picked up both books within seconds of Sacha putting them down.

"I could have lent you the Gautier, Sophie. Why didn't you ask me if there was a copy among the books at the tower?"

"You might not have wished to lend it."

"Not to everyone – no. To the granddaughter of a book collector – by all means. What have we here?" – turning to the second book – "*Travels with a Donkey*."

It was impossible to tell from his expression whether he

112

remembered their conversation the morning she had stormed up to the *torre* to take him to task for sacking Mike. But she felt certain he must recall it.

Fortunately Sacha chose that moment to say, "Sophie has told you about the trouble with the car, no doubt? It is possible the garage people are exaggerating the damage in order to make a big bill?"

"You've had an accident?" Carlos asked her sharply.

"No, no – we broke down merely."

"Where is this garage? I think I had better have a word with them," he said, at the end of her explanation.

"Oh, no – why should you be bothered?" she protested. "I'm sure they're not trying to swindle me. Why should they be?"

"Because the motor business is one big swindle," said Sacha cynically. "How can you know what they do, or what they do not do? You must believe what they tell you."

"In general, Spanish garages are extremely moderate in their charges. But the tourist season brings a good deal of extra business. I might be able to expedite the matter," said Carlos. "Did they give you their card, Sophie?"

"Yes, but I'm sure Sacha is worrying unnecessarily. If the car is not ready in time for our return journey – well, we can get back by bus, and I'll come and fetch it when it is ready."

"Nevertheless I'll have a word with them. The card, please – and a pen, if you have one in your bag."

Reluctantly she surrendered the card given to her by the garage proprietor, and unzipped the pocket containing her ballpoint.

"So you're staying in Granada instead of at a camp, as you intended. Where shall I find you tonight?" he asked.

She told him, and he wrote the address on the back of the card. The sight of his handwriting reminded her of the note which had accompanied the great basket of carnations he had sent her in Barcelona. The note which she should have torn up but which, betraying all common sense, she had kept.

Carlos then asked Sacha if he would like to hear some *flamenco* that night and, when the Frenchman assented, prepared to add his address to the one given by Sophie.

"It is the same. We are both at the Santa Clara," Sacha told him.

Sophie saw Carlos's eyebrow lift. She said, "It's perfectly *decoroso*. Sacha is sharing a room with two other young men, and I am chaperoned by the owner's youngest daughter. It was kind of them to squeeze us in. Granada is packed at the moment."

"I don't doubt the *respectibilidad*, only your comfort," he said dryly. He beckoned the waiter, and paid the bill. "I'll pick you up at nine o'clock. Come as you are. We will eat somewhere beforehand."

"I suppose he is staying at the Meliá or the Luz," said Sacha, referring to the city's most de luxe hotels, when Carlos had left them to finish their drinks at leisure.

"Probably." Sophie began to dip into *Travels with a Donkey*.

Presently, when Sacha asked if she would like another drink, she said, "No, thanks. If we're going to be out late tonight, I think I'll go back to the Santa Clara and rest. See you later."

In spite of its unprepossessing four-storey façade in one of the narrow side streets connecting two of the city's many smaller *plazas*, the Hostal Santa Clara was not as comfortless as it might seem to someone accustomed only to the biggest and best hotels.

The place had been recommended by the garage proprietor who was some relation to the owner, and although

114

it was not the sort of establishment in which Sophie would have chosen to spend a protracted holiday, for a long week-end it was both cheap and interesting.

After some conversation with the owner's wife in the café-bar on the ground floor, she climbed the four steep flights of stairs which led to the attic she was sharing with eight-year-old Concepción. Too small to contain any furniture other than two single beds with a shiny, gilt-handled chest of drawers, the attic was clean, and it did boast a modern hand basin. Only the cold tap worked, producing, after much gurgling and banging in the pipes, tepid water in a series of symphonic bursts rather than a steady stream.

After a top-to-toe wash with the lemon-scented Spanish soap she had used since her second week in the country, Sophie put on a short cotton wrapper which matched her best nightie, and lay down to read for an hour or two.

Before she had turned twenty pages, Concepción tapped on the door and came in to chatter, and to share a paper cone of *pipas,* the dried sunflower seeds which were cheaper and longer-lasting than *caramelos.*

Concepción's two eldest sisters, Elena and Dolores, and her brother Emilio, were working in hotels in England. Before she finished telling the family history, Sacha was at the door to enquire if Sophie felt like a stroll to the *churrería* on the corner.

Guessing that this suggestion would find great favour with Concepción, she asked him to wait while she dressed. Then the three of them went to the shop which specialised in *churros,* long fluted sticks of sugary doughnut mixture which tasted doubly delicious when dipped in cups of hot chocolate.

"Is he your *novio?*" asked Concepción.

Sophie shook her head and explained that she and Sacha merely worked together on the coast.

115

"Do you suppose her mother thinks we are betrothed, and will ask us to leave when she finds out we aren't?" she said to him.

"Why should she do that?"

"It's not like a big hotel where all kinds of irregular things go on" – the memory of the Miramar jabbed suddenly, like an exposed nerve – "and she might think I was a bad girl by Spanish standards."

Sacha laughed. "She is not so stupid," he replied, in his own language. "Anyone can see you are not anybody's girl." Carlos couldn't see it, she thought. Now that he was going out of her life – and she felt sure he did not mean to return to the *torre* again this summer – all the unhappy disillusionment of her arrival in Spain was being revived.

It was eight o'clock when they returned to the Santa Clara, and Concepción was called to the kitchen to help her mother to prepare the family's evening meal.

In spite of Carlos's parting injunction, Sophie did not mean to reappear in the pink cotton tunic-and-trousers suit she had worn for sightseeing. She went up to the attic and put on her favourite dress, the dress she had meant to wear to dine with him in Alicante. She had bought it in France. The colour of a lemon sorbet, it looked nothing on a hanger. But as soon as she tried it on, she had known it was worth every franc of the price.

At a quarter to nine, Señora Moreno came panting upstairs to announce that a gentleman "*muy hombre*" was awaiting Sophie in the bar.

On the way down, Sophie knocked on the door of Sacha's room, and called out, "Carlos has arrived."

She heard him answer, "I'll be there in five minutes. Okay?"

"Okay."

"That young man is also to escort you?" enquired Señora

116

Moreno, from half way down the next flight. She sounded disappointed.

"In England we have a saying that there is safety in numbers, *señora*."

The proprietress gave a screech of laughter. "Ah, very true – very wise! The one who is below is capable of making even a woman of my age behave foolishly. Such shoulders! Such magnificent teeth! His smile would melt the snow on the summit of Mulhacen," she exclaimed, rolling her eyes.

Carlos was listening to an old man without any teeth when Sophie entered the bar. The contrast between them was very striking; and yet perhaps, in his day, the old man had been every inch as *muy hombre* as Carlos.

She thought of El Gran Capitán whose name, long ago, had rung like a trumpet across Europe, but of whom now nothing was left but bone-dust and a painted effigy. For the first time in her life she was conscious of her own mortality, and the possible unwisdom of rejecting opportunities of happiness.

"Is something the matter?" asked Carlos, as they shook hands.

His percipience startled her. She said, "No, nothing," and wondered why he could read her expression so easily while his own was usually an enigma.

The same thought recurred some hours later when, replete after a long delicious dinner, they sat in a leafy garden watching a dark-eyed girl tossing her long black hair, drumming her scarlet heels and making her castanets rattle in rhythm with her feet. She was a beautiful, fiery-looking creature, and Sophie would have expected Carlos to watch her performance with the same look she saw on the faces of most of the other men present. But his grey eyes were oddly impassive, almost as if he were bored.

117

While the dancer rested from her exertions, a young man sang *cante jondo,* after which the girl danced again, flourishing the ruffles of her skirt, twisting and twining her white arms and sinuous hands, flashing her eyes and her teeth in the frenzy of *flamenco* at its fastest.

It was very late when they left the *carmen* where the performance had taken place. Carlos summoned a taxi. He sat in the back beside Sophie, with Sacha next to the driver.

Unlike London taxis, in which Sophie had often been kissed by William and others, the Granada taxis provided no privacy for lovers. Indeed the space in the back was inadequate for Carlos's long legs, and Sophie sat tucked in her corner to give him maximum room for them. Sacha's cigar and the taxi driver's pungent pomade made the air in the cab rather cloying. She was glad when Carlos wound down a window.

He said, "Tomorrow I'm spending a night at the *parador* near the top of the Sierra Nevada. As your car won't be ready for some days, Sophie, would you and Sacha like to come up the mountain with me, and I'll drive you both back to the coast the day after tomorrow?"

Until he reminded her of it, she had forgotten the car.

"Oh, dear, is the trouble something serious? What did the garage people tell you?"

"No, it's not too serious. Merely a part which they don't keep in stock and will have to order. I've arranged that, when the job is done, one of their lads will bring it back to camp for you. He can then hitch-hike back to Granada. There are always plenty of lorries on the main road from here to Motril. To give him a generous tip will be no more expensive, and less trouble, than coming to fetch the car yourself."

"It's very kind of you to have arranged it. I hope the part for my car doesn't take as long to arrive as the one for the

118

Dutch family's car," she said, rather worriedly. The people from Holland had been marooned at Torre del Moro for three weeks longer than their intended sojourn.

"I shouldn't think so," he said easily.

The taxi had reached their *pensión*. As he helped Sophie out, Carlos asked, "Well . . . do you care to see the snow at close quarters?"

"I should like to come."

"And you, Sacha?"

Sophie held her breath until Sacha said that he, too, would enjoy a night away from the heat for a change.

For fear that the overhead light would disturb Concepción if it remained on for more than the time it took her to undress and wash, Sophie did not read in bed, much as she wanted to find the passage Carlos had meant.

He had arranged to meet them for breakfast in the café not far away. During the course of this meal, Sacha discovered he had left his watch at the Hostal Santa Clara. He went back to retrieve it.

"What would you have done if Sacha had said he didn't want to visit the *parador*?" Carlos enquired, when they were alone.

She continued to spread peach jam on her roll. "I should have said, politely but firmly, that in that case I couldn't come either."

"In spite of my promise not to make any passes at you while I am in charge at the camp? You don't place much faith in my words," he said dryly.

"But you qualified that promise by saying 'unless you yourself indicate that virtue is no longer its own reward'. If I had agreed to come to the *parador* without Sacha, you might have thought I had changed my mind."

"I had forgotten that proviso."

"I hadn't." She was glad she was wearing dark glasses so

119

that he couldn't see her eyes and perhaps detect the ache in her heart. *Bliss was it in that dawn to be alive, but to be young was very heaven.* It was bliss to be having breakfast with Carlos, in the sun, in the legendary city of Granada. But if his smile had been tender as well as quizzical, if their mutual attraction had been mental as well as physical ... then it could have been 'very heaven.'

After breakfast they drove out of the city by way of the Plaza de Isabel la Catolica. It reminded Sophie of Piccadilly Circus except that here, instead of the little winged god of Love, the traffic swirled round a statue of Spain's greatest queen enthroned on the top of a plinth with fifty or more jets of water forming a horseshoe-shaped fountain below her.

Then, swiftly, the city was left behind and the road sloped up a wooded canyon leading into the foothills of the mountains.

Sophie had approved of Carlos's driving in Barcelona. Now, as the road began to coil in a succession of tight, steep U-bends, she was doubly impressed. Being a motorist herself, she knew that it was not easy to make the car swing smoothly round repeated hairpins.

When they had been climbing for some time, he stopped, and they all got out to look at the view. Although they were now at a great height above the city and the fertile *vega* beyond it, the dazzling whiteness of the snowfields was still far, far above them.

He had provided some elevenses. For Sophie and Sacha there was *vino tinto* and a cardboard box containing several different pastries. Carlos himself drank mineral water, and she remembered him saying long ago that he never drank wine when he was driving. Nor did he share the pastries. Wrapped in several paper napkins he had a thickly-cut *bocadillo* of fresh bread filled with something dark.

"That looks good," she remarked.

"I don't think you would like it, Sophie." His expression was sardonic.

"Shouldn't I? Why not?"

"You can try it, if you wish. Break off a piece." His eyes, as he offered it to her, were both challenging and mocking. Clearly there was something about the sandwich which he expected her to find obnoxious, and it was going to amuse him to watch her trying not to show her revulsion. What *was* in the sandwich? Something she *would* hate to swallow? Something to sear her throat for hours?

Not without a qualm, she broke off a small portion of crust and with it a slice of sausage resembling purple-brown marble. Cautiously she bit off a mouthful and chewed it, braced for unpleasant reaction.

"But it's delicious!" she said, in a puzzled voice, when she had swallowed it.

"You really think so?" he asked, with an oddly searching look.

"How could anyone not? What sort of sausage is it?"

"*Butifarra negra*. It's not a southern sausage although it is obtainable down here. It's a Catalan speciality. The bread has been moistened with olive oil and the juice from a tomato."

"And you thought I would hate the olive oil?"

"It's unusual for the English to like it well enough to want their bread soaked with it. This sandwich is what you would be offered as a snack in a bar used by Spanish workmen. I assumed you would prefer something of that sort" – indicating the rich pastries.

"Which just proves how unwise it is to have preconceived ideas about people," she replied, with a level look.

"You're right. After all, it isn't the first time I've misjudged you."

The oblique reference to the Alicante episode made her drop her gaze, and say quickly, "The pastries look equally delicious. I'll try this long one with the almonds on it."

Above the foothills, the mountainside was bare of all but low-growing scrub. With each swing of the road the air became cooler and crisper. At last, not far from the summit, they came to the *parador*, a long, low-lying building designed as a snug haven for skiers when the crags lay deep under snow.

When the reception clerk handed her a pen, Sophie again remembered the last time she had signed a hotel register, and the humiliation which had followed. She wondered if Carlos was also recalling the other occasion when they had booked in at the same hotel.

The clerk handed over their room keys, and Carlos picked up Sophie's overnight bag as well as his own. The three of them started to mount the stairs. Half way up, Sophie grabbed the handrail and leaned against the wall, breathing unsteadily.

"Don't be alarmed. You aren't ill. We're eight thousand feet above sea level. You can't gallop upstairs at this altitude – at least, not until you've adjusted," Carlos reassured her.

"What a horrid sensation!" she said, as her heartbeat slowed down.

"Sorry, I should have warned you." He handed her small case to Sacha, and put his arm round her waist to help her climb the remainder of the stairs.

"I also can feel the effect of this altitude," murmured Sacha, behind them.

"You'll survive," Carlos said cheerfully.

Glancing up at his face, Sophie saw by the laughter in his eyes that his arm was not round her because he thought she might not reach the top without it.

On the landing, she drew away from him. "Thank you. I'm fine again now."

Her room, she discovered, was on three levels. It was intended to accommodate four people, but evidently the number of guests staying at the *parador* at present was far short of the eighty or more guests which Carlos had said it could house.

The lowest part of her room had two bunk beds and a tiled bathroom. Several steps led up to a sitting area with a writing desk, cowhide chairs and a double window with a view down the mountain to the city. From this mezzanine, a longer flight of open pine stairs led to the highest level which had twin beds and another bathroom.

Sophie had a quick shower. She was wrapped, toga-fashion, in a luxuriously thick white bath sheet, when someone knocked on the door. She hurried downstairs.

"*Quién es?*"

"Carlos."

With her hand on the knob, she hesitated, wondering whether to call out that she was changing. Then, keeping herself behind it as much as possible, she opened the door, and said, "Yes?"

"Have I dragged you out of the bath?" asked Carlos, taking in her towel-draped shoulder.

"No, no. I was already out. Is anything the matter?"

"I thought you might be glad of this if you want to walk this afternoon. It will drown you, but it's better than nothing, and presumably you didn't bring any warm clothes with you?"

"No, I didn't. Thank you very much," she said, taking the sweater. "But what about you? Have you another to wear yourself?"

"Yes, I have all my kit in the car. I am only spending one more night at the *torre*, so I packed before I came

123

away. See you later." He disappeared along the passage.

Sophie closed the door, and shook out the rolled-up navy sweater. It was made of cashmere, with the silk label of an expensive shop for men in Zürich inside the neck. His thoughtfulness made her ashamed that a few moments ago she had been nervous of opening the door in case her *déshabille* prompted him to do something unnerving like coming inside and kissing her.

I wish I knew how far I can trust him, she thought, remembering their conversation at breakfast.

After lunch they walked up to look at the Virgin of the Snows, a tall modern statue, made of some silvery alloy, surmounting an arched cairn of stones between twenty and thirty feet high.

"Mulhacen and Veleta are the two highest peaks in Spain," Carlos said, later on, in answer to a question from Sacha. "Mulhacen is almost eleven thousand five hundred feet, which is higher than some of the peaks in the Swiss Alps."

Sophie remembered Señora Moreno remarking that he had a smile to melt the snow on Mulhacen. Cocooned in the warmth of his sweater, she could enjoy the breeze which made the clumps of rock-grass shiver, and would have made her shiver, too, had she had only her cotton shirt to cover her.

The sun was sinking when they returned to the *parador*. At Carlos's suggestion, they relaxed in the pine-beamed lounge bar on the gallery above the dining-room. The armchairs were covered either with rawhide or with grey and brown horse-blanket checks. The wall at the back of the gallery was hung with old-fashioned brass fire-irons which gleamed in the restful glow from the Spanish pottery table lamps.

The men drank beer and read newspapers. Sophie sipped

a glass of scalding-hot *cafe con leche,* and fell into a drowsy reverie. She must have slept for a little. When she opened her eyes, only Carlos occupied the sofa opposite her chair.

"Where's Sacha?"

"He's gone up for a nap."

"I think I'll do the same."

"Why not? The desk will call you if you tell them what time you want to be woken for dinner. We thought of eating about nine, if that's okay with you?"

"Yes, fine." She rose. "Don't get up."

But he was already on his feet. When, at the door, she glanced back, he had resumed his seat and was deep in a news magazine. Absurdly, she felt piqued that he had let her go so readily. She had expected him to suggest that she had another coffee, or a drink.

In her room, she had a long bath, and then lay on the bed and opened *Travels with a Donkey.* About half an hour later, she found the passage she was seeking.

'For there is a fellowship more quiet even than solitude, and which, rightly understood, is solitude made perfect. And to live out of doors with the woman a man loves is of all lives the most complete and free.'

To make sure she could not be mistaken, she read to the end of the book, but found nothing else which could be what Carlos had called "Stevenson's formula for the good life."

At a quarter past eight, her telephone rang. Someone said, in Spanish, "You wished to be called, *señorita.*"

"*Si ... gracias.*" Sophie replaced the receiver, and swung her legs to the floor.

Carlos was where she had left him when she re-entered the lounge a few minutes before nine. He was writing a letter. But he had been upstairs in the meantime. Now he was wearing a different shirt and trousers.

125

It was curious how sometimes he seemed very Spanish and sometimes very English. Tonight, by comparison with the Spanish men in the lounge who were all wearing suits and smelling strongly of after-shave, Carlos seemed extremely English. In Sophie's opinion, his casual clothes were far more suitable to the ski lodge atmosphere than the suits of the other men present, and she had long ago reached the conclusion that men should smell clean but not scented.

Dinner, like lunch, was excellent, with such lavish helpings of everything that, had they not spent the afternoon energetically, even Sophie's good appetite might have been unequal to the spit-roasted chicken which followed the inch-thick swordfish steaks.

"You're quiet tonight, Sophie," said Carlos, cocking one dark eyebrow at her.

For some time he had been listening attentively to Sacha, and she had taken advantage of his absorption to study him, and to wonder what had happened to change him from the boy in search of "solitude made perfect" to the worldly man who had long since discarded his youthful ideals – at least in relation to women.

"I'm dazed with mountain air and food," she answered, taking up her wine.

Carlos raised his glass to her. "*Salud y pesetas*."

"I would rather have health and . . . happiness."

It had been on the tip of her tongue to say "and love", but she had substituted happiness because in his vocabulary love did not mean what she meant by it.

"As you wish. *Salud y felicidad*." He drank to the amended toast.

After dinner, the two men played chess and Sophie idled through the pages of a French fashion journal left by someone, and sipped the refreshing blend of chilled orange juice and *champaña* which Carlos had ordered for her.

The day after tomorrow he will have gone, and I may never see him again, she thought, watching his sunburnt hand moving one of the chessmen. They were beautiful objects, carved from green and white jade. The box in which they belonged folded flat to form the chessboard. Perhaps he had inherited the game from the Spanish great-uncle who had left him the picnic hamper fitted with silver goblets and silver dishes.

I wonder what would have happened if I had been a different kind of person and had stayed with him at the Miramar, and had wired to Piet and Margriet that I wouldn't be coming? she speculated. I wonder if Carlos and I would still be together? Or if he would have tired of me already? At least now, when he leaves, I shall still have my self-respect. I shall be unhappy; but I shan't feel discarded and desperate, as Kate did when Richard ditched her.

No, but Carlos is not someone's husband. He is free, and you are free, and what harm could it have done to be happy with him? the other side of her argued. There'll be precious little satisfaction in remembering that you resisted him when you're Aunt Rose's age, and you've never met anyone else who meant a thing to you compared with Carlos.

At eleven she went to bed. The two men were still playing chess.

"I'm afraid we've neglected you," said Carlos, as he rose to bid her goodnight.

"Do you think women must be amused all the time, or they become bored?" she asked coolly. "I am capable of *thinking,* you know."

"My dear girl, I wasn't disparaging your intellectual resources but rather my own manners," he said dryly. "Have you something amusing to read in bed?"

"Yes, thank you. Goodnight. Goodnight, Sacha."

Annoyed with herself for being touchy, she left them.

But although she had Gautier's *Wanderings in Spain* to read, it failed to hold her attention. She could think of nothing but Carlos, and his imminent departure, and of how much she would miss him.

At seven o'clock the next morning, a flurry of hail against the glass made her jump out of bed to close the window. It was still showery when she went down to breakfast. Their table in the dining-room was empty, and she decided to go ahead with breakfast. The waitress brought coffee with toast, butter and peach jam, followed by a basket of *churros* and some sugary buns, served hot, which the Spanish girl said were called *zuizos*.

As she ate, Sophie watched shafts of sunlight breaking through the overcast sky. The weather seemed to be improving. Suddenly, for no reason that she could explain, she turned her head to look at the staircase which connected the dining-room with the gallery. Near the top of the stairs stood Carlos, motionless, watching her. She had the feeling that he had been standing there for some minutes. As their eyes met, he gave a nod of greeting and came down the staircase to join.

"Good morning. How did you sleep?"

"Like a log until the hailstorm. Have you noticed the quality of the sheets? They're Sea Island cotton."

"No, I can't say I've noticed the sheets." He sat down and unfolded his napkin, and the waitress brought him his coffee, turning the handle of the pot and that of the milk jug towards Sophie.

"She thinks we are married," said Carlos, turning them in his direction.

"Don't married people usually come down to breakfast together?" said Sophie, studying the crumbs on her plate.

128

"She thinks we have had a row. That is why you are frowning at the tablecloth instead of smiling at me as a good wife should at the breakfast table. Here she comes with my toast. You can see she is worried about us. It upsets her to feel that the guests here are not enjoying themselves."

"Then why not tell her that we're not married and we haven't had a row?" Sophie kept her eyes down.

He put his hand under her chin and tilted her face up. "Because it would be so much simpler for you to give me that lovely smile of yours."

His touch, and the tone of his voice, and the look in his eyes, made her heart pound even more wildly than it had on the stairs the day before.

Then the girl brought his toast to the table, and asked if Sophie wished for something more to eat, and the heart-plunging instant was over. A few moments later Sacha joined them.

Sophie stayed at the table until the two men had finished eating, but she took little part in their conversation. She was almost totally preoccupied with Carlos's inscrutable behaviour. *Why* had he given her that look? *Why* had he said her smile was lovely in that tone which could melt a hailstone?

As the three of them rose from the table, he said, "I thought that instead of returning the way we came yesterday, it would be more interesting for you if we went down the other side of the mountains."

"But I thought the road stopped at the top?" said Sophie.

"The tarred road does, but there is a road of sorts which would bring us to Capileira, one of the Alpujarra villages."

"What time do you plan to leave here?" asked Sacha.

Carlos glanced at his watch. "As soon as you're both

ready to go."

"I can be ready in ten minutes." Sophie left them to go to her room.

When, less than ten minutes later, she went down to the reception lobby, she was a little uneasy that Carlos might have paid her bill. To her relief, he had not.

The sky was a solid mass of cloud, and another hailstorm seemed imminent, when the white car slid out of the garage and headed for the summit of the mountain. The statue of the Vergen de las Nieves looked as grey as the dark clouds above her, her silver sheen dulled by the wintry coldness of the light.

At the highest point of the pass there was a notice warning motorists that the way down the seaward side of the Sierra was only suitable for small vehicles and Land Rovers, and that all drivers should proceed with extreme caution. Because, from this point, the road became a shale mule track disappearing between banks of snow, the effect of the notice was somewhat alarming.

To negotiate the sharp bend there, Carlos had brought the car almost to a standstill. Before he released the brake, he turned to Sophie and said, "If you don't like the look of it, we don't have to go down this way."

From the back seat, Sacha asked, "Have you travelled by this route before?"

"Yes, many times. It's tricky, but not really dangerous." To Sophie — "But if you don't trust my driving, you needn't scruple to say so. Or if you don't care for heights."

"I trust your driving completely," she assured him.

"Let's go, man. It looks an experience," Sacha agreed.

Carlos made the car move gently forward. "But only my driving . . . *verdad*?" he said quietly to her. Then he gave his attention to the passage ploughed through the snowfield.

The drive down took almost three hours, and in places

they passed through a rockscape of awesome remoteness and bleakness. The only habitation was a large, slate-roofed stone hut which Carlos said was the Refugio Rio Seco, a shelter for mountaineers. Occasionally the track passed a small tarn of icy green water. For much of the way they were driving along the brink of precipitous banks of shale which looked as if, at any moment, they might avalanche into the ravines below them. But although she would not have cared to take the wheel herself, Sophie had no doubt that Carlos knew what he was doing.

At last the bare and barren mountainside began to give way to turf and a few windswept bushes. Further down they passed a herd of black goats, and then a crude, comfortless house where a woman in black with a black scarf over her hair stared stonily at the car and its occupants.

Can she be happy? Sophie wondered. Even with Carlos I couldn't be happy living there. But perhaps if I had never known anything else . . .

They stopped for lunch by a rushing stream above the village of Capileira. Carlos put a bottle of wine and a bottle of Casera *mineral* in the stream to chill. Sophie wondered if he were about to produce the silver-fitted hamper. But the packed lunches put up by the *parador* included disposable plates and beakers.

Half a bottle of wine and the noonday heat made her feel very drowsy after lunch. Both she and Sacha were yawning as they climbed into the car. But Carlos, having drunk only Casera, showed no inclination to doze. The heat never seemed to affect him.

Afterwards, Sophie remembered Capileira as a huddle of old white houses with cascades of geraniums spilling over their balconies. Then the road wound steeply down, passing other, similar villages, through a countryside of woods and fields and vineyards.

131

Presently, in a somewhat larger township, Carlos parked opposite a café-bar.

"Coffee?" he suggested.

As they crossed the road towards the awning-shaded tables and chairs set out on the pavement, he said to Sophie, "I think you should find the *retrete* here reasonably civilised."

She appreciated his consideration although, if it had been necessary, she would have had no hesitation in disappearing into the undergrowth when the two men had done so at their picnic stop.

It was late afternoon when they reached the camp. Carlos dropped them at the entrance, and cut short their thanks with a casual, "I'm glad you enjoyed it."

Then the car shot away, and Sophie was left with a sinking conviction that the rest of the summer – perhaps for the rest of her life – was going to be a painful struggle to forget someone who would doubtlessly forget *her* in the space of a month.

After the quietness and luxury of her room at the *parador* the noise from the flats overlooking the camp was doubly disturbing. That night she slept badly, and woke with a headache.

About mid-morning she was comforting a small child who had tumbled down the wash-house steps when Sacha came by, and said, "Carlos wants to say goodbye to you. He's waiting outside your caravan."

"Oh . . . is he?" Sophie felt a kind of terror seize her.

"I will look after this one," said Sacha, going down on his haunches to talk to the child.

Slowly, Sophie made her way to the caravan, bracing herself for the effort to seem calm and unconcerned.

She found Carlos sitting in her camp chair.

"You're off, I hear. Have you a long run ahead of you?"

she asked brightly, as he saw her and rose to his feet.

"No, not very long."

"Well . . . *buen viaje*, Carlos." She held out her hand.

"Thank you." His hand enclosed hers and held it. And continued to hold it. "Actually I am hoping to persuade you to come with me," he said, after a pause.

"Come with you?" she echoed blankly.

"There's no need to tense," he said dryly. "I am not suggesting anything improper. It is merely that my cousins have a problem which you might be willing to solve for them. I telephoned Hilario last night to say I would be arriving at the *cortijo* this evening, and he told me that Miss Hempnall, the girl's governess, has had to go into hospital for some sort of minor operation. He thought I might know of an English girl to replace her for two or three weeks. I said I would ask you."

"But what about my job here? What about my car?"

"I have spoken to Piet. He's willing to release you. As for your car, it can be brought to the *cortijo* instead of here. In Spain such matters are not difficult to arrange."

The question she wanted to ask, but couldn't, was: "How long will *you* be staying at the *cortijo*?" Instead, she said, "Will Piet have me back when Miss Hempnall comes out of hospital?"

"I am sure he will, but it may be that Hilario and Luisa can find you a more interesting post if you want to prolong your stay in Spain. The job you have here is pleasant enough, I suppose, but it can only give you a very superficial impression of Spanish life. Wouldn't you like to discover the Spain behind the façade of *turismo*?"

"Yes, of course I should," she agreed.

It didn't sound as if he planned to stay at the *cortijo* for long. But even a few days more with him would be better than saying goodbye now.

"Then you'll come?"

"But I have no experience of teaching children," she said to postpone the decision a little longer.

"That isn't important. You can read to them, and talk to them, and generally keep an eye on them. Ordinarily my cousin would look after them herself while Miss Hempnall is away. But Luisa is pregnant again, and has to take life rather quietly during the early months."

"I see." Sophie drew in her breath. "In that case I'd be glad of the opportunity to see something of Spanish family life."

"Good girl." It was clear that Carlos had had little doubt that she would fall in with his proposal. "How long will it take you to pack? Half an hour?"

So it was that, about an hour later, she began her third journey along the coast road which led, eventually, to Cádiz. Little had she thought on the night when Carlos had fetched her back from Nerja that, before very long, she would be travelling with him to an unknown destination in the mountains far west of Málaga. Even now she could hardly believe that instead of saying goodbye to him, she had taken leave of Piet, Margriet, Sacha and the other staff at the camp. Nor was she any more certain that, in choosing to come away with him, she had made a wise decision.

"It's possible to veer inland at Málaga, but I propose to keep to the coast road until we reach San Pedro de Alcantara." From the pocket in the door on his side, Carlos extracted a Michelin and tossed it on to her lap.

Sophie opened the map and arranged it to show the whole length of the Costa del Sol from Almeria to Gibraltar. After some moments, she said, "The road between San Pedro and Ronda is marked with a string of red crosses. What does that signify?"

"*Estrada en muy mal estado* – a road in bad condition.

134

But don't let it worry you. It's a slow road, but not a dangerous one."

Whenever she heard him speaking Spanish, it caused her a curious pang in the pit of her stomach. It reminded her of the night he had kissed her, and murmured, *"Buenas noches, querida."* She felt sure that Spanish was the language in which he made love.

Thinking of Carlos making love, she began to daydream. In the car's capacious boot there were now four pieces of luggage; her fibreglass suitcase and smaller bag, and a large leather suitcase of his, and a stout canvas grip with hide handles. What unutterable bliss it would have been if, instead of being bound on their present journey, they were setting out on their honeymoon.

She was brought back to reality when Carlos touched his horn to remind a group of village children that they were playing on the edge of a main road. Aware of the folly of allowing her imagination to embroider an impossible theme, Sophie said hastily, "The way we came down the mountain from the Parador Sierra Nevada isn't marked on the map at all!"

The white car ate up the miles and, by Spanish standards, it was not too late for lunch when they drew up outside a restaurant near the fashionable resort of Marbella. They had not talked much on the way. Sophie had sensed that when Carlos drove fast he liked to concentrate. From her point of view there had been so much to see that talking would have been a distraction.

San Pedro was only a short way further along the coast and it was four o'clock in the afternoon when they turned off the highway at the junction with the inland road to Ronda. At first the steep, winding road reminded her of the route from Almuñecar to Granada. Presently she began to realise that the thickly wooded *serrania de Ronda* was far more remote and wild than the road she had motored along with Sacha.

As if he read her thoughts, Carlos said, "This used to be *bandolero* country. It's only a couple of decades since the police shot the last of the outlaws."

Once or twice he stopped the car, and Sophie was able to climb out and gaze in awed admiration at the deep, dark-shadowed ravines and distant, desolate-looking heights. The road and the car seemed incongruous in a place otherwise unchanged for centuries, a place meant for eagles and wild boar, not for people. For nearly two hours they drove further and further into the wilderness, and all the time the sun was losing its heat, and the light was becoming more mysterious.

When at last they came to the top it was to a region of moorland which reminded Sophie of *Wuthering Heights*. Here Carlos again stopped the car, and walked back to unlock the boot. As he did so, faintly, from a distance, Sophie heard the plaintive clonking of goat bells. But of farms or cottages or people there was still no sign. And now the sun was sinking low, and very soon it would be dark.

"You had better have my sweater again," said Carlos, handing her the jersey she had returned to him the day before.

He shrugged on a brown leather jacket, then stood with his hands on his hips, looking about him. A breeze had sprung up. It ruffled his well-brushed black hair, and the sunset light burnished his tan to the colour of bronze. In the collarless coat of soft leather, with his dark shirt open at the neck, it needed only a cloak slung back from his shoulders to complete the illusion that he was not the Carlos she knew but a stranger from another century, a man who, once, had belonged in this wild, haunted high country. And as she thought this, her eyes on his arrogant profile,

136

there came back to her all the romances she had made up about him years ago; and how, in those adolescent fantasies, recurring theme had been the night ride to the mountains. Which now, in a way, had come true.

Perhaps Carlos felt her staring at him. He returned to the car and climbed in. But instead of switching on the engine, he lounged in a sideways position, one arm crooked over the ledge of the open window, the other stretched along the backrests. It was now her turn to be scrutinised.

"How much further have we to go?" she asked, her voice slightly strained.

"Not very far. Are you tired? Would a little brandy revive you?"

"Oh, no, thank you. I'm not at all tired." For the sake of something else to say, she added, "This is very isolated, isn't it? Not the sort of place one would want to break down or run out of petrol . . . or anything."

Carlos said nothing to this and, after a moment, the quality of his silence made her flick a rather furtive glance at him. He was still watching her intently, and the look in his eyes was one she had never seen in real life, but had often imagined on his face. A hundred times, in past daydreams, she had conjured precisely that blaze of hot-blooded ardour.

"I see it has suddenly occurred to you that my cousins may be merely decoys, and that I am no longer bound by that promise I made you," he said, in a bland voice.

As a schoolgirl, she had found it exciting to imagine herself in the power of a ruthless but attractive man. In reality, she discovered, such a situation was anything but enjoyable.

CHAPTER FIVE

CARLOS leaned towards her, his arm sliding down from the backrest to circle her shoulders. "All this time, and still I have not kissed you," he said, in Spanish. "Amazing!"

Sophie strove to sound cool and relaxed. "But you've kissed me twice, Carlos," she pointed out, speaking English.

He drew back a little, puzzled. "Twice? When?"

She retrieved her mistake by saying quickly, "Well, almost twice. Once in the lift in Barcelona. And I think you intended to kiss me when I slipped on the path from the tower the night we had dinner with you."

He laughed, and the arm round her tightened. "Perhaps ... but you ran away. As for Barcelona, you don't call that a kiss, do you? It was merely a friendly goodnight. This time, however –"

At the same moment that Sophie closed her eyes, the first hoofbeat sounded on the road. Seconds later the animal was in view, a large scrawny mule straddled by a rustic Spaniard who peered at the occupants of the car with unabashed curiosity.

He was not alone. There were two other riders behind him. They must have come over the moorland, the turf and low, heathery brush muffling the sound of the mules' huge, ungainly hooves which seemed to splay in all directions be fore they clashed on the macadam.

As they crossed the road near the car, Carlos bade the riders good evening. They responded, shouting remarks in thick Andaluz which, to Sophie, was incomprehensible.

"You see we are not as isolated as you thought," Carlos said dryly, starting the engine.

Round a bend in the road they met a boy with white plastic chaps over his trousers and a stick in his hand.

"Goatherd," he added succinctly.

Further on, a bus was setting down passengers who hurried across the moorland towards some great crags. "They are people from Igualeja coming home from the day's work in Ronda."

It was twilight now, but the plateau had lost its eerie atmosphere. Sophie felt ashamed of letting her imagination run away with her. How could she have thought for an instant that Carlos was capable of engineering a situation in a which, if not literally trapped, she would be dangerously vulnerable?

For the rest of the way they were seldom out of sight of a farm, its lime-washed walls catching the strengthening moonlight.

"Is Mrs. McKinlay still staying with your cousins?" she asked.

"No, Tía Jacinta has gone back to Scotland, and Mari-Luz is also away at present. But you'll soon make friends with the others."

"I hope so."

"Of course you will," he said confidently. And, a little later, "Here we are."

As he slowed down to turn the car between two tall gateposts, she caught a glimpse of a ceramic tile set near the top of each pillar and painted with an emblem, and the words *cortijo de Cupril*. The emblem, she discovered later, was the brand on the Marqués's cattle.

The *cortijo* was a long way from the road. From outside it had a forbidding appearance. All the windows were guarded by heavy grilles, and shuttered as well. The massive door was studded with six-inch iron discs. It was more like a fortress than a farmhouse.

Carlos tugged the bell pull, and almost at once the wicket was opened by a manservant who bowed to Sophie, and then explained to Carlos that the family were in Ronda at a function, but would return within the hour.

She, meanwhile, was gazing in surprise and pleasure at what lay within the thick outer walls of the building. In front of her was a screen of intricate wrought iron through which, as if through black lace, she could see a tiled court-yard with a fountain and a full-grown fig tree. On the opposite side of the *patio*, a staircase led up to a gallery with many doors opening off it.

A few minutes later, conducted by a shy little maid in a black dress and white muslin apron, she was on her way to her bedroom on one side of the gallery, and Carlos was being shown to his room on the other side.

When they arrived, the courtyard had been lit by moon-light and two or three lanterns. But when Sophie came out of her bedroom, bathed, changed and rested, the foliage of the ancient fig tree was glowing with dozens of fairy lights, and garlands of lights festooned all sides of the *patio*. Beneath the tree, a large table was laid for dinner, and several immaculate children were chattering together by the foun-tain.

As she descended the stairs, the children saw her and fell silent. And then for the first time she noticed that Car-los and an older man were seated in chairs which until then had not been visible to her.

"Sophie, may I present my cousin Hilario?" said Carlos, when she had joined them.

Later, the introduction puzzled her. Considering that she was to work for him, and he was a Spanish aristocrat, she would have expected to be presented to the Marqués.

"You are very welcome, Miss Lingwood. I hope we can
140

make your visit here an enjoyable one," her host said, as they shook hands. "My wife wishes me to apologise for her absence from the table tonight. As you have heard, we have been to a ceremony in Ronda, and Luisa is now rather tired. You know, I believe, the reason why she is easily fatigued at this time?"

"Yes, Carlos has explained," she said, smiling.

He was not at all like her preconception of a *marqués*. He was short and rather stout, with hair no darker than her own, and a friendly, rather weatherbeaten face. There was nothing of the haughty *hidalgo* about him. He looked more like a farmer or a fisherman.

The children were waiting to meet her. There were six of them, four boys and two girls, all so neat and clean, and so formal, that Sophie was slightly unnerved by them.

When their father had told her their names, and each child had bowed or curtsied, Carlos said quizzically, "They are not always like this. Wait till you see them tomorrow before you decide they are too perfect for this world."

Later that night, when the younger children had disappeared, and only the two eldest boys were quietly playing chess on the other side of the *patio*, the Marqués said, "Tomorrow, unfortunately, I must return to Seville. And you, Carlos? What are your plans? Are you pressed by matters of business, or can you stay for some time?"

Sophie held her breath in the pause before Carlos answered.

"I can stay for some days," he replied. "Next week — who knows what may happen?"

"Very true. Who can say?" agreed his cousin. Soon afterwards he said goodnight to Sophie, and went up to chat to his wife, taking his sons with him.

"Can you ride, Sophie?" asked Carlos, in the silence which followed their departure.

141

She shook her head. "I'm afraid not. Will it make me a rather poor substitute for Miss Hempnall?"

"Not at all. I shouldn't think she rides either. I asked because it's a convenient way to reach some of the places of interest round here. But they can also be reached by Range Rover."

He rose from his chair and went to switch off the lights in the branches of the fig tree and along the cornice beneath the balustrade of the gallery. This left the patio moonlit, for the lanterns had been extinguished earlier by the servants.

As he came back to where she was sitting, Sophie wondered if now he intended to carry on from the moment when the clatter of mules' hooves had stopped him kissing her.

When he said, "It's been a long day. I expect you could do with an early night," she was not sure whether to be disappointed or relieved.

Rising, she asked, "What time does the day usually start here?"

"Early. But don't worry about oversleeping. One of the maids will call you in plenty of time to bath before breakfast. Goodnight, Sophie."

"Goodnight." Aware that he was watching her, and wishing she knew what he was thinking, she mounted the stairs to the gallery.

On her first morning at the *cortijo*, she was woken by goat bells. When she climbed out of bed and went to the window, she could see the herd grazing on a distant hillside. But the air was so still that the bells did not sound far away. Presently, the shepherd began to sing. She stood motionless, listening. This, she thought, is the real Spain. Benidorm and Torremolinos are no more typical of Spain than Southend and Blackpool are typical of England. Some people like those crowded places, of course, but I would much rather have these quiet, open spaces.

As she leaned on the sill there came the whinny of a horse and the sound of hooves on paving somewhere below her. Then Carlos came into view, riding a beautiful black horse, with a stiff-brimmed grey Cordobés hat tilted over his eyes.

It must have been only by chance that he turned to look up at her window. Seeing her, he swept off his hat.

"Good morning. You're awake early."

"Good morning. The goat bells woke me." She was conscious of the transparency of her nightgown. Her aunt had made it for her from a length of sheer white voile embroidered with delicate sprays of Ayrshire work. It was cool to wear and very pretty. But it was not a garment in which to take to the lifeboats, or to talk to a man like Carlos. Yet to draw back inside the room seemed ungracious when he was bringing his mount close under her window.

To her surprise, Carlos, usually so observant, seemed not to notice her flimsy covering. A few minutes later he was riding away towards the hills, leaving Sophie to ponder the difference between his manner in the car the previous evening, and just now when he had appeared as indifferent to her femininity as if it had been a nun or a schoolgirl to whom he was speaking.

She turned from the window and went to look at herself in the large mahogany cheval-glass. Her hair was loose on her shoulders, and a little rumpled. Her cheeks were still flushed from sleep. The nightgown veiled her brown skin, but did not entirely conceal the places where her tan began and ended. She guessed that, from a man's point of view, she looked more attractive now than when she had put on her face, and brushed her hair, and was dressed.

It was possible, perhaps, that Carlos had ignored her

déshabille out of politeness. But although she could imagine him respecting the modesty of an old woman or a very young one, somehow it did not seem probable that she herself, whom once he had meant to seduce, was all at once, overnight, to be treated with rigid propriety.

But propriety, or rather a kind of sexless friendliness, was the treatment she received from Carlos during the next few days. She began to feel that she must have imagined that blazing look in the car before the muleteers passed them.

On the second day he took her, with the children, to Ronda to see the famous ravine dividing Ciudad, the old town, from Mercadillo, the new town. Ronda had an eighteenth-century bullring, but Sophie was more interested in the market where for a few pesetas Carlos bought a large bag of saffron to send to the wife of a friend in England. The keeper of the spice stall gave all the children, and Sophie, a spoonful of tiny aniseed-flavoured sweets like hundreds and thousands. Some minutes later she was amused to notice two black-clad old ladies receiving the same treat.

Presently, passing a bakery, Carlos bought a dozen *bandilleras*. As they drove home, they crunched the long crisp sticks of bread named after the darts used in bullfighting.

Another day they went to El Burgo, a village not marked on the map, where Carlos stopped the car for them to watch a row of six mules endlessly circling a threshing floor to reduce straw to the fine *paja* with which they were fed. Sophie had already noticed some *paja*-stacks and, puzzled by their likeness to giant-sized tin loaves, had meant to ask what they were, but had forgotten.

In El Burgo she saw for the first time the woven grass awnings called *toldos* stretched across the streets from roof to roof to give areas of shade in which elderly villagers sat and gossiped, falling silent when the strangers passed among them.

"If you live here, even Ronda is a big, wicked city," murmured Carlos.

But although he was amused by the stares which followed them along the cobbled street, Sophie sensed that his Spanish heritage meant more to him than she would have suspected at one time.

His favourite village was Montejaque, an uphill straggle of terraced houses leading to a small, tree-lined *plaza* with, on one side, a manufactory of mountain hams and *chorizos*. There he bought a large ham to send to the recipients of the saffron. Unexpectedly, he knew a great deal about the cuisine of his mother's country, and it was from him that she learned that in Spain the so-called Swiss roll was known as a gypsy's arm, and the idiom for leftovers was "old clothes."

That was the day of the picnic under the cork oaks. After the visit to Montejaque, where women still carried buckets Moorish-fashion on their heads, and did their laundry out of doors in small wooden cradle-shaped troughs, he drove the Range Rover into the countryside and found a place where, but for the road passing through and the bark-stripped trunks of the trees, civilisation could have been a hundred miles away.

For the children there was a huge hamper packed with all kinds of good things made by the Marquesa's cook. But Carlos had his own ideas about picnics, and very soon the delicious aroma of onions, and of fresh bread frying in olive oil, was wafting past Sophie's nostrils.

"Inés says that bread and oil is only fit for very poor people, and that we should be ashamed to be seen eating such a thing," remarked Juana, referring to one of the housemaids.

"Inés is a snob," answered Carlos, slicing one of the large, oddly-shaped tomatoes which, as Sophie had discovered, were far more subtle in flavour than the smoothly rounded tomatoes commonly sold by English greengrocers. "When she is older and wiser, she'll know that if a thing is good, it's good for every sensible person, whether they're rich or poor."

He caught Sophie looking thoughtfully at him. "You'll share my lunch, won't you, Sophie?"

"If there's enough for me."

"Ample."

While they were eating, a large herd of young cattle came past, driven by two mounted men, and with one big brown cow, with a bell round her neck, in their midst. Their hides had the gloss of black satin, and Sophie was suddenly struck by the beauty of the scene around her, the pale gold of the dry grass, the matt orange trunks and grey-green foliage of the trees, and the hot blue sky overhead.

Now, at this moment, I'm happy, she thought, drinking wine. When I am old, I'll remember this day and this place.

But then the younger horseman made a detour to say good-day to her, and when she saw how he looked at her it reminded her that Carlos had stopped looking at her in that way. Indeed, when the meal was finished, he did not even bother to chat to her, but lay down to have a siesta.

The children had already wandered away to explore, but she remained on her camp stool, gazing at the distant hills until she judged that Carlos was dozing, and it was safe to gaze at him instead.

He was lying on his back on the rug, one leg drawn up at an angle, one forearm shading his eyes. The other arm was outstretched, and she was suddenly filled with a powerful yearning to stretch out beside him and rest her head on his shoulder, and to feel that strong arm close round her, and to go to sleep in the sun.

... to live out of doors with the woman a man loves is of all lives the most complete and free ... solitude made perfect.

The drone of a heavy vehicle broke the peaceful silence Carlos stirred and sat up, and Sophie fixed her eyes on the blue gleam far down the road. It was the lorry's plastic visor which, catching the sun, gave off that bright sapphire light. It was part of the essence of modern Spain, like the black silhouettes of the bulls which were the trademark of a popular brandy, and the airline hoardings proclaiming "With Iberia you would have already arrived", and the black-clad traffic police on motor-bikes, always riding in pairs, one ahead of the other.

Another memorable expedition was when Carlos took them to see the Cueva de la Pileta. Sophie expected the cave to be similar to the famous cave at Nerja where Carlos had come to find her when she had chosen not to return to the camp with Mike.

But this cave, near the hill village of Benaojan, was very different from the commercialised one on the coast with its café and gift shop and park for several hundred cars.

Here, once they had passed above the red rooftops of Benaojan, the track climbed a parched brown mountainside and finally stopped at an area where cars could turn round, and perhaps five or six could park. From here a steep path led upwards to a flight of rocky stairs. At the top was a hole in the cliff, barred by a stout iron grating. This, at present, was standing open, and a pleasant-faced Spaniard was beside it, waiting for them.

"Ah, Don Carlos, so it's you. It's some years since we last saw you."

The men shook hands, and Carlos introduced the Spaniard as a farmer from the valley below. He and his brother

147

looked after the cave, discovered by their grandfather in 1905, and guided visitors through its galleries to the innermost limit, two kilometres from the entrance.

Because Carlos was known to the Bullon family and, as a boy, had explored the cave many times, his party did not need to be guided. He and Joaquin carried the paraffin lanterns which were the only source of light, and Carlos led the way up the steps of the Hall of Bats into the great Central Nave where the first of the prehistoric cave paintings were to be seen.

Sophie was fascinated by the paintings, one of which depicted a mare in foal, another a long-horned goat. The most curious drawing was that of a fish. The underground pool called The Bath of the Moorish Queen was interesting, and so were the patches of smoke-blackened rock above the places where the cave dwellers had burned their fires. But when they came to the great abyss, which Esteban said was more than two hundred feet deep, she was seized with an irrational fear of the things which might lurk in those black unimaginable depths.

"Tio Carlos has climbed to the bottom on a rope," Esteban told her admiringly.

"You haven't?" Sophie exclaimed, in horror, to Carlos.

"Certainly. Why not?"

"I wouldn't go down for a fortune," she said, with a shiver. "How dreadful for the people who lived in here to have that pit yawning beside them."

He raised the lantern a little, and looked closely at her. Then he took her hand in his free hand, and gave it a squeeze, and said cheerfully, "I expect it made a useful rubbish dump. Come on, *niños*, time to go home."

Even with her hand in his, the way back to the entrance was an unpleasant experience which made Sophie thankful to emerge into the bright, hot outer air once more.

Later, when the children were not within hearing, Carlos said, "I think I should keep out of small caves in future, if I were you, Sophie. I wouldn't have taken you in there if I'd thought you would find it disagreeable."

"I'm sorry. I know it's stupid. Suddenly I – I felt the roof might cave in," she admitted reluctantly.

"So I guessed. Your hand was like ice, and clammy, which could only mean a bad attack of jitters. It's nothing you need be ashamed of. You did very well not to let the *niños* know how you felt."

But afterwards, although he had been very understanding and nice about it, Sophie felt she must have sunk in his estimation. If a man was as interested in caves as Carlos evidently was, surely a girl who was frightened of them must seem a tiresomely nervous person?

It was in Ronda that they met Antonia. She came over the bridge from the old town, a dark, vivid girl in white trousers and a yellow shirt, with a white bag slung at shoulder blade level, and sun goggles tinted sea-green and rimmed with silver which flashed in the sun as she turned her head this way and that.

A few yards before they drew level, she stopped in her tracks, and cried, "*Carlos!*"

"Hello, Antonia. How are you?" He addressed her in English, except for pronouncing her name in the Spanish way, Anto – *nee* – a, accentuating the third syllable.

"I *was* bored – but not now," she replied. "For how long are you here? *Don't* say you're leaving tomorrow. I couldn't bear it." Her English was almost as perfect as his, but she had a strong Spanish accent.

"No, not tomorrow. My plans are rather indefinite. Sophie, this is Antonia Llobera. We have known each other since childhood."

149

As the girls shook hands, Sophie was conscious that although Antonia's manner was not unfriendly, she would have preferred to meet Carlos when he was unencumbered by nephews and nieces and a foreign girl.

She linked her arm with his, and said, "The house has been full of all my aunts and uncles, talking of nothing but their health. Now they have gone away, and Papa has retired to his library. You must come and amuse me, Carlos. When can you dine?" She produced a small leather diary. "I have an engagement tonight, and also tomorrow. But Friday is free, if that suits you?"

"Yes, but perhaps I had better consult Luisa before accepting. She may have some plans she hasn't yet mentioned, or which I have heard but forgotten. I'll send you a note," said Carlos.

Antonia permitted a wrinkle to mar the smoothness of her forehead. "When is Hilario going to allow a telephone at the *cortijo*? I would find it impossible to live without it.'

"Hilario would find it impossible to escape the workaday world if he had a telephone. I consider it's very sensible of him. Any messages of real urgency come by telegram to Ronda, and are then delivered to the *cortijo* by special messenger."

"But think of poor Luisa, unable to gossip with her women friends. And it can't be convenient for you to be out of touch with the world. Only this morning Papa had to telephone London about some book he must have."

Later, on the way home, Carlos told Sophie, "Antonia's father is a retired diplomat who now devotes most of his time to his collection of bindings. He and your grandfather would have a good deal in common."

He then dropped the subject, and Sophie forgot the remark until the following Friday, during lunch, he said, "By the way, Sophie, in my note to Antonia I mentioned

150

that you were the granddaughter of a distinguished English bibliophile, and Señor Llobera is looking forward to meeting you tonight."

"But *I* know almost nothing about bindings – at least not the kind of fine bindings which he would consider collectable," she protested.

"No matter. I'm sure you'll listen to him more appreciatively than most of Antonia's guests, and you'll pick up plenty of material for your next letter home."

"Yes, it will be an interesting experience for you, Sophie," the Marquesa agreed. "The Llobera house is not like this. It is a town house, a small *palacio,* very old and with some magnificent furniture."

Later, when she was dressing, Sophie wondered if Carlos had arranged to take her with him so that she could talk, or rather listen, to Señor Llobera while Carlos concentrated on Antonia.

She had zipped up her dress, and was wondering whether to wear ear-rings, when the Marquesa came to her room.

"Yes, I like that very much," she announced, after a critical appraisal of Sophie's expensive French dress. "It is plain, which is always more becoming than the flowered dresses of which the English seem so fond. Our good Miss Hempnall always wears flowers in the evening, and they do not flatter her figure or her complexion." She noticed the open jewellery case on the dressing-table and came closer to see what trinkets her visitor possessed.

"Ah, these are charming. You should wear them tonight," she said, picking out the pair of small pearl drops which had been Sophie's father's wedding present to her mother. "But I see they fasten with screws. Why don't you have your ears pierced? It is so much more comfortable, and also there is then no danger of losing one's valuable jewels." She examined a scarf pin which had belonged to

151

Sophie's grandmother. "This also is very pretty. I have always liked these blue stones. *Turquesa* ... what is that in English?"

"Turquoise." Sophie watched her pick up a locket and, not for the first time, admired her beautiful manners.

She knew that Doña Luisa had jewels compared with which her own few ornaments were little better than the rubbish in Christmas crackers. Yet the Marquesa's interest in Sophie's bits and pieces was neither assumed nor condescending.

"At one time we thought Carlos and Antonia Llobera would marry," remarked the Marquesa. "In some ways it would have been suitable. But Carlos has a difficult temperament. It is not enough for him that she is handsome and healthy and, because her mother is dead, is also experienced in the arrangement of a household. No, Carlos looks for something more – but what it is, I don't know. Perhaps you understand him, Sophie?"

"I? Not – not at all. Why should I understand him, Doña Luisa?"

Her hostess gave a little shrug. "Sometimes I think it must be the English side of his nature which is the difficulty. The English have this belief that always one must marry for love, even when, in all other ways, the two people concerned are extremely unsuitable together. No doubt you also believe in love – yes?"

"Yes, I do; but I don't think that *real* love leads people into unwise marriages. Physical attraction can certainly do so, but real love is quite a different matter because then the mind is involved as well as the body," answered Sophie, with conviction. "I wouldn't have thought that Carlos believed in true love," she added, in a carefully casual tone.

Before the Marquesa could reply, there was a tap at the door. When Sophie called, *"Adelante"*, the door opened a few inches, and Carlos said, "Are you nearly ready?"

"I am here with Sophie. You may enter," said his cousin.

He came into the bedroom. Noticing Sophie's dress, he said, "I thought you would wear your white dress, and the cloak you showed Tía Jacinta."

She looked at the Marquesa. "Will Señorita Llobera be wearing a long dress? Is this too informal?"

Doña Luisa looked at Carlos. "You did not say it was to be a large party. I thought there would be only the four of you."

"Yes, as far as I know there will be."

"Then why should Sophie wear a long dress? This pale yellow one is most suitable."

"And very attractive," he agreed. "I wasn't being critical, Luisa. It was merely that I expected to see her dressed as she was in Barcelona." He glanced at his watch. "It's time we were on our way."

On the gallery, by the head of the stairs, the Marquesa wished them both an enjoyable evening, and went to her room.

The white car was outside the entrance, and as Carlos closed the passenger door he looked down at Sophie and said, "Anyway, I prefer you with your hair down, and it was the way you smiled at me that night, not your dress, which I remember most clearly."

This sudden reversion to his former manner, after days of detached friendliness, took her by surprise.

"Is that an example of a *piropo*?" she asked, as he slid behind the wheel.

"That's for you to judge, *señorita*," he said, in Spanish. As he switched on the engine, she saw that he was smiling.

But during the drive he talked about Spain, and of his belief that in the 1980s his mother's country would be a leading member of the European Economic Community.

153

And as she listened, Sophie reflected that he had not talked to her like this when they dined together in Barcelona, or during the weeks at Torre del Moro. The fact that he thought she would be interested in his views on the future of Europe pleased her more than that he remembered what she had worn at their first meeting.

The Lloberas' palatial house was the dominating building in a village not unlike Montejaque and Benaojan. Within it was like a small museum, and although she saw much to admire Sophie felt that, as a home, it did not compare with the *cortijo*.

However, there was nothing stiff about Señor Llobera. They had scarcely been introduced before he whisked her away to his library to see some of his treasures before dinner.

Antonia and Carlos did not accompany them immediately, but joined them some ten minutes later.

"Oh, Papa, you should be ashamed," Antonia scolded him. "You have been so busy showing your books that you have forgotten to give Miss Wingfield a drink, and now it is time to eat."

Carlos cocked an interested eyebrow at the *Historia de Alexandre*, bound in blind-tooled dark green morocco, which his host had been showing to Sophie. But Antonia steered them firmly in the direction of the dining-room. However, even if it bored her, she was too good a hostess to try to divert the two men from discussing their great mutual interest, and to Sophie, who had long wanted to know about Carlos's collection, the conversation during dinner was absorbing. More than once she had to repress a comment which would have revealed her personal interest in the subject.

It was not late by Spanish standards when she and Carlos took their leave.

"I'm afraid it's been rather a dull evening for you girls. If we were nearer the coast we could go on somewhere, but round here there are only *bodegas* and even Ronda has no sophisticated night life," he said, as they left the outskirts of the little town behind them.

"It wasn't a dull evening for me. I enjoyed it immensely. Although I shouldn't care to live in such grandeur," Sophie said candidly. "Are they here all the time, or only in the summer, like your cousins?"

"Only in the summer, although I fancy Don Salvador will live here all year after Antonia's marriage."

"She's engaged?"

"Yes, but it hasn't been announced yet. She has finally found someone who meets her somewhat exacting standards – and who doesn't share her father's passion for books. She thinks one collector in the family is more than enough," he said dryly.

"Some women don't mind being collectors' wives. My grandmother didn't."

"She was a rarity. Most women do resent any interest which excludes them – unless, of course, they happen to have one of their own. The ideal wife for a book-collector is a book-collector, but the females of the species are so few, and generally not very alluring when they are discovered" – on a wry note.

It was a remark which called for a careful reply, and Sophie was weighing her answer when Carlos swore and wrenched the car off the road. There was nothing else he could do to avoid a head-on collision with the car which had burst into view, coming fast on the crown of the road with no lights to warn of its approach.

Afterwards, Sophie wondered what would have happened had they not been held by the safety belts. She felt sure she would have been flung out and perhaps severely

155

injured. Mercifully the side of the road at the point where they catapulted off it was a low stony bank sloping to a fairly flat expanse of thorny scrub. A single boulder in their path would undoubtedly have overturned the car. As it was, they suffered no more than several seconds of violent rocking and jolting before coming to rest with the bonnet nudging a prickly pear bush.

"Are you all right?" Carlos unlocked his seat belt and quickly released Sophie from hers.

"Y-yes . . . yes, I think so," she answered unsteadily.

"Raving maniacs! They damn nearly killed the lot of us," he said furiously. "My God, if I was near a telephone. I'd have every *guardia* from here to Seville on their track. But it's at least a couple of miles to the nearest farm, and they won't have a telephone."

"Why didn't those people have their lights on? Because the moonlight is so bright, and they didn't expect to meet any other cars, do you think?"

"God knows? Judging by their speed, I should think they were either drunk or drugged – maybe both. All I do know is that we'll be uncommonly lucky to get this car on the road again."

He was right. One of the front wheels were so badly buckled that the car would have to stay where it was until rescued by a breakdown truck.

"How far from home are we?" asked Sophie. "About fifteen miles?"

"Yes, and ten from the Lloberas' place. Too far to walk back to them. We shall have to put up at the farmhouse on that ridge" – pointing to it – "and even that won't be easy walking for you in those shoes. I wonder if by any chance . . ." He left the sentence unfinished, and went to open the boot. "Yes, Esteban has left his tennis kit in here, including his shoes. They won't be a good fit on you, but better than high heels for rough walking. Sit down and I'll put them

156

on for you."

Sophie had been standing by the car. Now, obedient to his command, she opened the nearside door and perched sideways with her feet on the ground.

As he crouched to unbuckle her flimsy sandals, she saw the black trickle of blood down the side of his face.

"You're hurt!" she exclaimed.

"Hurt? No, I'm okay."

"But you are, Carlos. Look!" Gently, she touched his lean cheek and showed him the stain on her fingertips.

"A thorn branch must have caught me. It's only a scratch. In the heat of the moment I didn't even feel it happen." He pulled out a handkerchief and blotted the side of his face. "Here, let me wipe your fingers or you may soil your dress." He took hold of her hand and wiped the ends of her fingers. "You're cold, *pobrecita*. Put this round you." Quickly, he stripped off his jacket and wrapped it about her shoulders.

"I'm not really cold. It's just shock. I'll be all right in a minute. You need this as much as I do."

"Don't argue, there's a good girl." He returned to the task of changing her shoes. Surprisingly, his hands felt normally warm.

It was about three kilometres across country from the damaged car to the nearest farmhouse, and most of the way Carlos kept her hand tucked in his so that, long before they reached the *cal*-washed farm buildings, she had lost her feeling of horror at their narrow escape from a fatal crash and was almost grateful to the driver of the other car for causing her to be stranded with the one person with whom it was not a trial but an adventure.

"Are you intending to ask them to lend you their car?" she enquired, as they approached the farm.

"They probably have only four-legged transport, in

which case we may as well spend the night here. Hilario is an early riser. When he finds out we haven't come home, he'll come to look for us. The car will lead him to this place."

No glimmer of light showed through the shuttered windows of the farm, and when Carlos had rapped several times on the door and they had waited for three or four minutes without receiving any hint that the knocking had been heard Sophie began to think the occupants must either be deaf or had no intention of disturbing themselves for whoever might be abroad at such a late hour.

Then, so suddenly that she jumped and gasped, the shutters of an upper window were flung open and the barrel of a shotgun glinted in the white light of the moon. A harsh, suspicious voice barked a question.

For some moments after Carlos had explained their predicament, the person continued to aim the gun at them. Then as suddenly as the shutters had been thrust apart, the gun was withdrawn and they were instructed to wait while its owner came down to let them in.

"Nobody is going to catch this old fellow napping," said Carlos dryly, as they listened to several bolts being pulled back to the inner side of the stout door.

The man who opened the door and beckoned them into the lamplit passage had several days' growth of white stubble frosting his wrinkled mahogany-brown cheeks. Although unshaven, he looked clean and not unfriendly. His lack of teeth made his country dialect impossible for a foreigner to follow, but Carlos had no difficulty in conversing with him.

Presently he led them upstairs to a room which, to Sophie's astonishment, was dominated by a large and exceedingly elaborate brass bedstead. Otherwise the room was hung with so many religious pictures and crucifixes that it was more like a chapel than a bedroom.

The old farmer opened a cupboard containing much linen, and said something which Carlos interpreted as, "You're to help yourself to the necessary sheets and pillowcases. Now that his wife is dead, a woman from the village keeps the place in order. He knows nothing about the housekeeping, but thinks you will find all you need."

While he was translating, the farmer opened a drawer and took out a folded garment which he placed on top of the chest.

"You can wear one of his wife's nightgowns," Carlos explained. "Do you think you can sleep in this atmosphere?" he added, eyeing a gruesome picture of a saint being martyred.

"At least there's no danger of the mattress being damp, which it probably would be in an isolated farmhouse in Scotland or Wales," said Sophie valiantly. "Your room may be even gloomier."

"I may be expected to share our host's bed," he said, with the flicker of a grin.

The old man lighted the lamp belonging to the bedroom. He then picked up the other lamp, bade Sophie goodnight, and ushered Carlos from the room. She heard them returning downstairs and listened to the sound of their voices until somewhere below the door closed and there was silence.

The sheets, when she spread them, smelt of rosemary. The nightgown of thick cream calico, soft from much washing, enveloped her from throat to toe. The long sleeves were edged with coarse cotton lace at the wrist, and the same lace trimmed the high collar.

She had opened the shutters and was standing at the window, gazing at the silvered landscape, when a tap on the door made her start slightly.

"*Adelante.*"

Carlos came in with an earthenware mug in his hand. "The

159

old boy has brewed a *tisane* for you."

She sniffed the hot steaming liquid. "Do you know what is in it?"

"Don't worry; it isn't an infusion of goat's droppings," he said, with a smile. "It's made from dried orange blossom, which is a well-known country sedative in Spain."

"Oh ... it's scalding," she said, after a sip. "I'll have to let it cool a little. I hope the old man won't mind my opening the shutters. It was so stuffy in here."

"Mm, and that nightgown wasn't designed for coolth," he remarked, eyeing the yards of material shrouding her tall slender figure.

The mug was too hot to hold. She placed it carefully on the sill, and said, "What shall we do if Don Hilario doesn't come to find us tomorrow morning? Is there a bus service on this road?"

"I shouldn't worry about that. Hilario will be here before you are even awake," Carlos said confidently.

She said, without stopping to think, "Yes, if he suspects an accident. But mightn't his first thought be that we hadn't come home for another reason?"

"What other reason?" His voice was clipped, quite different from his previous easy tone.

She began to wish she had not given voice to her thought.

"Well, he doesn't know me very well, and he must know that you ... that in the past –"

"You mean that is what *you* would think, knowing me as you do?"

"No, I didn't mean that. Only –"

"Even now you don't trust me," he cut in. "You never will trust me, will you? I could treat you like a brother for months, and still you'd be half on your guard with me."

"That isn't true –" she began.

But he wouldn't listen. He was angry, with a fierce hot

160

anger she had never seen in him before. His eyes no longer looked grey, but as dark and cruel as the eyes of the Moors in his ancestry.

He said softly, "The old man thinks you are my *novia*, but he has straitlaced Spanish ideas about that relationship. If I don't return to the kitchen in a matter of minutes, he will come up here with that shotgun and march me down. Meanwhile, as you are determined to distrust me, I may as well justify your fears." And he swept her into his arms and began to kiss her, not in the manner of a man kissing a girl for the first time, but as if she had belonged to him for years, as if they had been separated for months past, as if in a moment he would swing her off her feet and carry her to the great brass bedstead.

Before Sophie had adjusted to this onslaught, Carlos had flung her away and slammed out of the room. She heard him run down the stairs, and another door close with a bang, after which, for the second time that night, silence fell upon the farmhouse.

She was roused by sunlight on her face, and for a few moments she lay with closed eyes, aware of being hot and uncomfortable and in an unfamiliar bed. Then she remembered where she was and realised that the voluminous nightgown, ruckled round her waist, was the cause of her discomfort. She peered at her watch. It was nine o'clock. But considering that it must have been two o'clock in the morning before she had fallen asleep, it was not surprising that she was late in waking.

When she had climbed out of bed, her first thought was to find the privy. She dressed and quickly combed her hair. Then she went downstairs.

The sound of two men speaking Spanish led her to the kitchen, but when she pushed open the door, which had been ajar, it was not Carlos who rose from a bench by the table, but one of the elderly menservants from the *cortijo*.

"*Donde esta* Don Carlos?" she asked, when they had said good morning.

"He has already gone to the airport, *señorita*. Don Hilario instructed me to wait until you woke up, and then to escort you home. In this case are some of your clothes, and the necessities for your toilet."

"Oh ... thank you," said Sophie automatically. "But I don't understand; when did Don Carlos leave here? And why has he gone to the airport? Which airport?"

"The airport at Málaga, *señorita*. As to the reason, I cannot say. No doubt Don Hilario will explain that. Nor do I know at what hour Don Carlos left this place. I can tell you only that Don Hilario instructed me to fetch you, but not to disturb you as you would be very tired after the unfortunate accident you experienced last night."

"I see," she said dully. That Carlos should have left without seeing her was unbelievable. She was gripped by a terrible dread that this really was the end of their stormy acquaintance; that she would never see him again.

"Paco, could you ask the old man where the *retrete* is, please?"

The man consulted the farmer, then turned to her with a deprecatory shrug. "The facilities here are very primitive, *señorita*. The *retrete* is beyond the barn. The old man will conduct you there. Meanwhile I will see that there is hot water and a basin in your room when you return."

Within an hour Sophie was back at the *cortijo*, but neither the Marqués nor his wife were there to relieve her painful uncertainty. They had gone to Ronda to attend some important civic function and were not expected back until lunch time.

When they did return, they were both full of concern

162

that she should have had such a frightening experience during her stay with them.

"You will be glad to hear that the people in the other car have been caught," Don Hilario told her. "I am told that a group of young foreigners were arrested by the police in Torremolinos yesterday. They are suspected of possessing and perhaps selling drugs and, as you know, the authorities here are determined to protect our own young people from these evils. The courts which deal with contraband have the power to impose severe fines."

"Yes, sometimes thirty thousand pesetas or more," the Marquesa put in approvingly.

"But that is not all," continued her husband. "After the contraband court, such persons are charged with breaking the public health laws. For this, which is a criminal offence, the shortest sentence is imprisonment for six years. Therefore one understands why those ruffians in the other car would try to escape in the night if they also feared soon to be arrested."

"I see," said Sophie. "So that's why they had no lights on. To attract as little attention as possible. Though I should have thought that, at the speed they were going, the noise alone would have alerted people."

"Now they will also be charged with driving in a dangerous manner, and causing much damage to Carlos's car."

"Won't the police want a statement from Carlos? Won't he have to come back to give evidence?"

"Very possibly, but for the moment his most urgent business is with these poor people in Mallorca, some of whom were less lucky than you and Carlos last night."

"Mallorca?" she said blankly.

"You have forgotten, Hilario, that Sophie knows nothing of this," Doña Luisa reminded him. She turned to the English girl. "Very late last night we heard that fifty English

163

tourists had been hurt in a very bad accident on a coach excursion to a pearl factory in Mallorca. They have been staying in an hotel which belongs to Carlos, and he has gone to the island to see what help he can give. To have someone who speaks their language is a great comfort to people who are in hospital far from their own country."

"When I found Carlos at the farm, we came to your room to tell you this," the Marqués explained. "But you were so deeply asleep that he would not have you disturbed."

"I see," said Sophie, for the second time. But whereas the fate of the car-load of fugitives was of only minor interest, the discovery that Carlos's sudden departure had no connection with the incident in the farmhouse bedroom was of the greatest possible relief to her.

She said, "He can have had practically no sleep."

"He will have slept on the flight to Valencia, and from there to Palma. He has great vitality, but also he has the ability to relax himself. Many men – including you, Hilario – would be angry about the damage to the car, and that would prevent them from resting," said the Marquesa. "Carlos is different. If something bad has occurred, he will not brood on it. He has only to open one of his treasured old books and all his cares are forgotten."

It was a statement which at one time would have been equally applicable to Sophie. But in the days that followed nothing could distract her for long from thoughts of Carlos.

She remembered how, when the old farmer had aimed his shotgun at them from the upper window, instantly Carlos had stepped forward, placing himself between her and the menacing-looking barrel.

She remembered how, earlier, after she had touchd his thorn-torn cheek, he had said, "You're cold, *pobrecita*," a

Spanish colloquialism which meant "poor little one" and which, in the tone he had used, had sounded like an endearment.

Above all, she remembered being kissed. Again and again she relived the moments in his arms until, at the very instant when she was ready to free her arms in order to hold him as closely as he was holding her, he had thrust her away and stormed out.

On the second afternoon after the accident, a policeman came to the *cortijo* to take a statement from Sophie. He came in plain clothes, and she saw him arriving from her window and thought for a moment that it was Carlos coming back.

At dinner that night, the Marquesa said, "Perhaps tomorrow we shall have news of Carlos."

. But it was the fourth day after the accident before Don Hilario received an airmail letter from Palma. He read it, and passed it to his wife, who in turn passed it to Sophie. It was a laconic account, written in Spanish, of the aftermath of the coach disaster on the island. Carlos made no reference to the other accident, or to Sophie, or to when he expected to be able to return to his cousins' house.

From then on she began to doubt that he would return. When six days had passed without her receiving even a postcard from him, she felt that he would not come back. For surely if he had any regard for her, and any regret for his rough treatment of her, he would have found time to write a note, or arrange for some flowers to be delivered to her?

On the seventh day, while she was spending the siesta writing to Aunt Rose, one of the maids came to her room to tell her that Don Hilario wished to see her at once in the Marquesa's *tocador*.

Puzzled by this summons at an hour when, normally, the household did not stir, Sophie put on a dress and went quietly but quickly along the gallery to the door of Doña Luisa's pretty green and white boudoir. It was only when she had been bidden to enter, and saw the expressions on their faces, and the *telegrama* in Don Hilario's hand, that a terrible fear shot through her.

"*Not Carlos?*" she exclaimed involuntarily.

"No, no, it does not concern Carlos," the Spanish woman assured her, rising from the chaise-longue. "It is a cable from your family, Sophie. You are needed at home." And she took the cable from her husband and gave it to Sophie who read: SORRY TO TELL YOU GRANDFATHER SERIOUSLY ILL. DOCTOR THINKS RECOVERY UNLIKELY. IS IT POSSIBLE FOR YOU TO COME HOME? LOVE. ROSE.

It was a bad shock but, much as she loved her grandfather, the news that his long life was ending was not the appalling blow which, just for an instant, she had expected to receive. If Carlos had met with an accident ... if Carlos had been gravely ill ... even to think of it was agony.

Doña Luisa steered her to a chair and made her sit down, and Don Hilario patted her on the shoulder and said, "There is a flight leaving Málaga tonight. I am sure, in the circumstances, we can arrange a seat for you. By midnight you will be in England."

"But the children ... How will you manage?" said Sophie to Doña Luisa.

"Oh, that is of little importance compared with this sad news for you," the Marquesa replied, with a wave of one graceful white hand. "Come, I will help you to pack, and then Hilario will drive you to Málaga. It is very unfortunate that Carlos should be away at this time. If he had been here, he could have gone to England with you."

"I hardly think he would do that," Sophie said dryly.

"Anyway, I'm accustomed to flitting about Europe by myself."

"Yes, I know. But it is more enjoyable to have a man to look after one, don't you agree?"

"Sometimes."

Sophie remembered the expedition over the Sierra Nevada, and how Carlos had lent her a sweater, organised packed lunches for the drive down, cooled the wine in a stream and, later on, for her benefit, stopped at a café where the *retrete* was clean and pleasant. Oh, yes, it was far more enjoyable to have a considerate escort on all one's travels. Only now she had the sinking feeling that on all future journeys the comforts would have to be of her own making. Because it was going to be a long, long time before she stopped loving Carlos, and perhaps she never would be truly heart-free again.

She caught the flight to London with half an hour to spare. But during that time it was not possible to speak to her aunt on the telephone because of delays on calls to England.

The Marqués insisted on waiting until her flight was announced, and was deeply concerned that she would have no one to meet her.

"It doesn't matter, Don Hilario. As I told your wife, I'm quite used to travelling by myself, and it isn't a difficult journey from Gatwick to my home." Sophie was grateful for his kindness, but wished he did not feel obliged to stay with her. She would have preferred to be alone.

It was sunset when the aircraft took off with a load of cheerful Midlands holidaymakers, three empty seats, and one silent, grave-faced girl who sank into her seat and closed her eyes.

As the plane soared above the coast and veered northwards, Sophie was remembering some lines by the Spanish poetess, Rosalía Castro.

Happiness, I shall never find you again on earth, in the air, or in the sky, even though I know that you exist and are not an empty dream.

CHAPTER SIX

"Would Miss Sophie Lingwood on Flight 103 from Málaga go to the Information Desk where there is an urgent message for her. Would Miss Sophie Lingwood ..."

As the voice on the public address system repeated the announcement, Sophie guessed that during her hours in the air Don Hilario must have managed to get through to her aunt on the telephone

When she made herself known to the girl on duty at Information, she was told that Mr. Edward Hapton was coming to meet her, and was expected to reach the airport within fifteen minutes of her own arrival.

Who is Edward Hapton? Sophie wondered, as she sat down to wait for him.

Twice during the flight from Spain she had re-read the most recent letter from her grandfather. Nothing about it had warned her that it might be the last he would send her. The handwriting was as steady as ever; the news it contained as cheerful as always.

She was reading it again when a voice said, "Sophie Lingwood?" and she looked up to find a man with thick springy grey hair and dark-rimmed spectacles standing beside her.

"Yes, I'm Sophie. Are you Mr. Hapton?"

"Call me Edward. I'm a very old friend of your aunt's, and as she doesn't want to leave your grandfather's bedside, she thought you wouldn't mind if I came to meet you instead."

"How is Grandplum ... my grandfather?"

"Not too good, I'm afraid. It seems that his heart has

169

been in bad shape for some months, but he managed to hide it from Rose until last week when she found him collapsed in his chair. He rallied after some injections, but it was only a temporary recovery. He's been sinking gradually ... it's only a matter of time now."

"Yes, so I gathered from the telegram. I – I just can't imagine home without Grandplum," said Sophie, with a quiver in her voice.

Edward picked up her suitcase, and tucked his other hand under her elbow. He was one of those comfortable people with whom it was possible to feel at ease immediately, and Sophie was thankful that he was not a shy man or a hearty one. She was too tired to cope with a difficult person.

It was only when he was unlocking his car that she remembered her own car.

"What's the matter? Left something on the plane?" he asked, hearing her smothered exclamation of dismay.

"No, it's worse than that," she said wryly. "I've left my car in Granada. Until this minute I never gave it a thought. Oh, dear, what an awkward situation!"

"Never mind. I expect it's get-overable," Edward said calmly. "How is it that your car is in Granada if you have been working near Ronda?"

Sophie explained the reason. "I shall have to wire the Dutch people for whom I was working at first. Piet can probably find someone to drive the car back to England for me."

"Possibly, although I fancy there might be difficulties in connection with the insurance cover. Surely the simplest solution would be to fly back and fetch it yourself? Your present employers will be expecting you back in due course, won't they?"

"No ... no, I don't think so. They were not my employers in the usual sense. I was standing in for their children's English governess while she was in hospital. They are cousins of the man who owns the camping ground where I was employed, and he arranged for me to stay with them. But I shouldn't think the governess will be away for much longer, and as far as my original job is concerned . . . well, I don't want to go back to Spain unless it becomes unavoidable."

"You didn't care for the country?"

"I wouldn't say that. But the nicest parts of Spain are not places where foreigners can find work easily. The tourist areas, where there are jobs to be had, are terribly overcrowded and noisy during the season."

"If you like peace and quiet you ought to try my country – New Zealand."

"What brought you to England?" she asked.

"I came here eight years ago, after my wife died. I'm an architect, so it isn't too difficult for me to transplant myself. But for some time now I've been hankering to go home. My roots went deeper than I realised. It was only because I'd lost Margaret that I felt the need to get away from all the reminders of our life together."

"You had no children?"

"Yes, two. But, like you, they were restless youngsters and had already left home. Now my son is settled in the States. My daughter's married to a Scot, but they live in Italy." After a short pause, he added, "I met your aunt when she was commissioned to work an altar frontal for the chapel of a new teacher training college for which my firm were the architects."

Sophie remembered the altar frontal. He and her aunt must have known each other for more than four years. Why had Aunt Rose never mentioned him?

"Do you live near us?" she enquired.

"At weekends, yes. From Monday to Friday I'm in London."

When they reached Cliff Court, Rose Steel must have heard the sound of wheels on the gravelled drive. Before they had time to climb out, she was silhouetted in the doorway, waiting to give Sophie her customary warm hug of welcome.

"How is he?" asked Sophie, when they had kissed each other.

Her aunt drew her into the hall. "He died about half an hour ago."

Mr. Wingfield had bequeathed his house and income to his daughter, and his books to his grandchild. Their value was considerable, and he had left a note telling Sophie to have no compunction about selling the collection.

"No doubt Rose will wish to move to a smaller and more modern house when I am gone, and you may have difficulty in accommodating your own collection," he had written.

It was painful enough to lose Grandplum, and at a time when she needed his wise counsel more than ever before; the prospect of losing the peaceful book-lined room overlooking the sea, the room which all her life had been the very essence of "home" to her, made her sorrow doubly acute.

In the days that followed his death Sophie spent many hours curled on the window seat, longing to pour out her heart to the one person in the world whom she could have told about Carlos. Fond as she was of her aunt, she could not confide in her.

On the day after the funeral, Sophie was in the kitchen preparing a salad lunch when Rose came in, and said, without any preamble, "Edward has asked me to marry him."

Sophie turned a startled face to her. Since the night of her arrival from Spain, she had given no further thought to the reason why Rose had never mentioned the name of a man she had known for several years. Edward had attended the funeral, but they had not seen him during the interim. Presumably he had been in London.

Before her niece could say anything, Rose went on, "I've been fond of Edward for some time, but I was never sure if, as far as he was concerned, it was only a pleasant friendship between two lonely people."

"Have you been lonely?" Sophie asked. Her aunt had always appeared to be completely contented with her busy life.

"Not seriously lonely ... but a little," Mrs. Steel admitted. "There's a great deal of truth in the saying 'What you never have, you never miss'. Had I never been married, I don't think I should have been conscious of anything lacking. My work has been wonderfully satisfying, and I'm sure a child of my own wouldn't have given me any more pleasure and pride than you have done, Sophie dear. But I was married once, for a short time, and so there has always been a slight sense of incompleteness. I suppose I've noticed it more since you've been grown up. Father and I got on with each other very well, but I was never as close to him as you were. There was no intellectual bond between us. With Edward I do feel a mental bond because, basically, we are both designers."

"When did he ask you to marry him?"

"About an hour ago. After the funeral yesterday, he asked me to go for a walk with him this morning. Apparently he's been fond of me for a long time, but he knew I would never leave Father, and that Father was too old to have his life turned upside down."

"I suppose it was because of Grandplum that you never talked about Edward."

"Yes. Father was a very shrewd person. If he had known

173

about Edward, he might have suspected my feelings, and felt himself to be a burden on me."

"I would have looked after him willingly."

"Yes, I know you would, my dear. But it would have been wrong to ask it of you. Young people need a few years of freedom before they have any ties on them."

Privately, Sophie thought that if Grandplum had known of his daughter's wish to marry again, he would not have minded engaging a housekeeper to replace her. His books had been necessary to him, but he had never been possessive with people.

Aloud, she said, "When are you thinking of getting married?"

"As soon as possible, if Edward has his way. He says we've waited long enough as it is. But there is one big snag..." Her voice tailed off uncertainly.

"Which is?"

"Edward intends to go back to New Zealand soon. He's a widower, you know, and he only came over here because at the time he couldn't bear to go on living in the places where he and his wife had been happy together."

"Yes, I know. He told me about it the night he fetched me from the airport. But why is that a snag? Do you dislike the idea of living in New Zealand? Are you worried that you won't be able to carry on your work as well there?"

"Oh, no, I feel sure I shall like the country very much. As for my work, I should think there must be some scope for a professional embroiderer there. If there isn't, or if there's less scope ... well, one can't have everything in life. It's you I'm concerned about, Sophie. What's to happen to you? What we hope is that you'll come with us."

Sophie was silent, digesting this new turn of events.

"You could at least try it for a year," Mrs. Steel went on anxiously. "I know you're more than equal to looking after yourself, but even so it doesn't seem right to leave you on your own in Europe with no one of your own to turn to in an emergency. It would be a different matter if *you* were contemplating marriage. But you're not at the present time, are you?"

Sophie shook her head. "Maybe I will come with you," she answered thoughtfully. "Not as part of the household, but to have a look round the country, and to be within visiting distance if *you* feel a bit homesick at first. You might, you know. You're not a born gypsy like me." She paused. "The trouble is my only qualification is my languages. I don't know how much use they would be to me in New Zealand."

"Surely polyglots can find employment anywhere?" her aunt said, looking more cheerful. "Can you stretch that salad to three? I told Edward I wanted to break the news to you on my own, but that he could join us for lunch. I'll go and telephone him, shall I?"

After lunch it was Sophie's turn to go for a walk. The day was unseasonably chilly, and as she trudged along the almost deserted beach, from time to time turning her back to a flurry of sand blown up by the sharp north-east wind, it seemed to her far longer than a week since her departure from the warmth of southern Spain. Already her tan had faded. In another week it would be gone, unless the weather improved.

When she returned to Cliff Court, Edward and Rose were having tea.

"We've been talking things over, and Edward thinks it would be wiser to let this house, rather than sell it," said Mrs. Steel, as she poured a cup of tea for her niece.

"I'm sure that property values must continue to rise," added Edward, offering Sophie a buttered scone. "And as Rose doesn't need the money, it would seem more sensible to hang on to the place and perhaps convert it into flats. Then if, in a year or two, you want to come back to this country, you would have somewhere to live and a bit of income from the other flat."

That evening he insisted on taking them both out to dinner, firmly quashing Sophie's protests that she would be happy to stay at home and that it wasn't usual to celebrate an engagement with a dinner *à trois*.

"Nonsense! We aren't a pair of youngsters. We should like to have you with us," he insisted. "There's still a lot to discuss."

It was during dinner that he said, "By the way, Sophie, have you made any move to recover your car from Spain yet?"

"No, not yet. I was thinking about it this afternoon. Perhaps, in the circumstances, there's not much point in trying to have it brought back to England. Perhaps Piet could arrange for it to be sold. I'll write to him first thing tomorrow. And I must get in touch with Sotheby's and fix up the sale of Grandplum's books," she added, trying to sound casual.

She was glad when the evening was over, and she could retire to her bedroom and surrender to the despair which she had to hide during the day. The prospect of going to New Zealand did nothing to lift her spirits. She had no doubt that it was a country of great beauty and variety, but Edward said the European settlers had not gained a proper foothold until Victorian times, and Sophie found it difficult to work up any enthusiasm for a place where there would be no eighteenth-century houses, no mediaeval churches, no centuries-old olive groves, and – according to her *Directory of Dealers* – only a handful of antiquarian booksellers.

I'm a European, she thought miserably. I want to stay where I belong.

But she knew that if she refused to go with them it would be a weight on her aunt's mind. Apart from that consideration, to go far away to a new life was probably the best cure for her unhappiness.

Next day the weather was worse. Watching the breakers lashing the shore, Sophie felt sorry for any bad sailors who had to cross the Channel that day. Travellers with Hovercraft bookings would be delayed until tomorrow. The Seaspeed service did not operate when the sea was as rough as it was this morning.

After breakfast her aunt had to keep an appointment with her dentist. Sophie wrote the letter to Piet, put it on the hall table to post later on, and went to the kitchen to make a fruit flan for their supper. The flan case was in the oven, and she was draining a can of apricots when the front door bell rang.

The man waiting in the porch was looking at the wild sea when she opened the door. As he turned to face her, she gave a choked sound of disbelief.

"Hello, Sophie," said Carlos. "I've brought you your car."

It was at this moment that Rose Steel returned, staring in astonishment at the vehicle parked in the driveway. As she mounted the steps, she said, "That's *your* car, isn't it, Sophie?"

It was Carlos who answered, not her niece. Sophie was still dumb with shock.

"Yes, it is. Are you Sophie's aunt?" he enquired.

"Yes, and you must be one of her Spanish friends. How do you do?" They shook hands and she led him into the hall. "Sophie dear, do shut the door. The draught is enough to blow one's head off. Let me take your coat, Señor . . . er . . .?"

"I'm Carlos Walsingham."

"Oh, you're English. I'm sorry. I assumed –"

"I'm half English" – shrugging off his raincoat. "Do I gather that Sophie hasn't mentioned me?"

"Well, no," – with an uncertain glance at her niece – "but we have been in rather a turmoil since she came back from Spain. You see, my father – Sophie's grandfather – died last week, and –"

"Yes, I saw the notice in the *Telegraph*. I'm sorry. I'd looked forward to meeting him," Carlos said gravely.

"Sophie, take Mr. Walsingham up to the drawing-room, and I'll go and make some coffee," said Mrs. Steel. "And put a match to the fire. Mr Walsingham's hands are like ice."

Slowly, like someone hypnotised, Sophie did as she was told. As she straightened from lighting the paper and kindling under the logs, she said in a low, hoarse voice, "Where is your car?"

"It's at the *cortijo*. Hilario will have it shipped to me. I thought you might need yours urgently. Fortunately there was a convenient cancellation on the boat from Bilbao to Southampton. We docked at seven this morning, and I came straight here."

"Oh, Carlos!" she said, in a whisper. There could be only one reason why a man accustomed to driving a custom-built, air-conditioned, fast car should travel the whole length of Spain, in high summer, in a cramped, slow and badly sprung runabout. The heat of the central sierras must have been appalling.

"It was *you* I needed more than anything. I've been so unhappy . . . thinking I'd never see you again."

His arm, which had been resting on the mantelpiece, fell to his side. He seemed even taller than she remembered, his face strangely stern.

"Are you telling me you love me, Sophie?"

A deep flush swept up from her throat, but she did not

178

look away. "Yes," she said simply. "Yes, of course I do."

He took her face between hands still cold from his journey. But his lips were warm as he kissed her softly on the mouth. For some moments Sophie was passive, still stunned by this sudden reprieve from an unwilling voyage across the world to a life without hope of real happiness. Then she slid her arms round his neck, and clung to him with all her strength.

"Oh ... I'm sorry, I didn't realise –" murmured Mrs Steel, coming into the room with a tray, and discovering that her niece and their visitor were locked in a passionate embrace.

They drew apart, looking at her with dazed expressions. Carlos was the first to recover himself. As he crossed the room to relieve her of the laden tray, he said, "I'm afraid this may come as a shock to you, as Sophie has omitted to mention me, but we are going to be married."

"Yes ... it does seem a little sudden," said Mrs Steel, rather faintly "H-have you known each other for some time?"

He set the tray on the table close to the sofa. Then he went back to where Sophie stood, and put his arm round her waist. "How long have we known each other, *querida*?" Amusement glinted in his eyes. But before she could answer, he added in an almost angry tone, "If I'd had any sense, we would have been married by now."

"I see. Well ... what a surprise! So you won't be coming to New Zealand," Mrs Steel said, sinking into a chair and then rising again as she remembered that the coffee was waiting to be poured.

"No, I shan't. I'm sorry, Aunt Rose, I would have told you about Carlos, but until today there wasn't anything to tell. I – I knew how I felt about him, but not how he felt about me. We were rather like you and Edward."

179

In the hall, the telephone rang. Mrs. Steel hurried to answer it.

When she had gone, Sophie said, "Why didn't you *write* to me? All that time after you'd gone ... not a line ... not even a postcard."

"After what had happened at the old man's house after the accident, I thought a letter from me was likely to be torn up unread."

"I liked what happened that night. If you'd held me for a few more minutes, you'd have realised that I liked it."

"Would I? The impression I took to Mallorca with me was that I'd wrecked my chances for good. When I got back to the *cortijo*, hoping it might still be possible to put things right between us, you were no longer there. Then Luisa told me that when the telegram came about your grandfather, you seemed alarmed in case it was about me. She said that in her opinion you liked me in spite of everything."

"Liked you!" Sophie exclaimed. "If she knew what a struggle it was not to show how much I loved you. I hardly dared even to glance at you in case Doña Luisa began to suspect the truth."

"She knew all along how I felt. I had to tell her I wanted to marry you in order to persuade her to send the governess on holiday for a few weeks."

"On holiday! But I thought Miss Hempnall was in hospital?"

"No, I'm afraid the 'minor operation' was merely a subterfuge. It was the only way I could get you to myself for a while, and try to convince you that I wasn't such a bad type after all. Luisa and Hilario were not very keen on the deception, but eventually they yielded to persuasion. If you think back, you'll realise they never referred to Miss Hempnall being in hospital. They said only that she was 'away', which was the truth."

"But as soon as we reached the *cortijo* you seemed to become quite indifferent. As if you had even lost interest in a casual relationship."

He drew her into his arms. "I wanted you to feel safe with me. Do you remember the evening we drove up into the mountains from the coast?"

Sophie nodded "You were going to kiss me in the car, but some muleteers came past and you didn't."

"And you thought that perhaps we weren't on our way to my cousins, but to some secluded spot where, if you again refused to join my 'harem', I might toss you over a precipice – or threaten to," Carlos said dryly.

"Something like that did cross my mind," she admitted ruefully.

"Exactly: and as I was becoming extremely tired of being regarded in that light, it seemed best to assume an appearance of marked indifference. Which, as the *niños* were constantly running off and leaving us alone together, was far from easy," he added.

Sophie leaned her head against his shoulder, and gave a deep sigh of relief and happiness. "Never mind: I feel safe with you now."

His arms tightened, but then Mrs. Steel came back and unhurriedly he let Sophie go.

While they were having coffee, she explained about her aunt's impending marriage, and how the house was to be converted into flats and her grandfather's books sold at Sotheby's.

"Wouldn't you prefer to keep them?" asked Carlos, rising from his chair to cast an appreciative eye along the shelves.

"Yes, of course I should. But is it possible? They take up a great deal of room."

He turned and gave her a look which made her catch her

breath.

"If you want it, and I can arrange it, anything is possible," he said. "Until we find a house we like, they can go into store with my main collection."

"You could keep this house if you wished," put in Mrs. Steel.

But Sophie shook her head. "No, I always loved coming back here, but I don't *belong* here any more." She smiled at Carlos. "I belong with you from now on."

His expression did not alter, but his eyes were suddenly brilliant with controlled emotion. If her aunt had not been in the room he would have come to her and kissed her. Indeed it was not very long before Mrs. Steel did find a tactful reason for absenting herself; and then, within seconds of the door closing, Sophie found herself being made love to in husky Spanish.

Eventually, he said, in English, "We must be married at once because I think you have lost your powers of resistance, *querida*, and for me it is even more difficult. Is there a register office here? Let's go and enquire about a special licence, and also I must buy some shirts. There wasn't room in your car to bring all my luggage."

It was late in the afternoon, at the end of a crazy, happy shopping spree, that they happened to pass the windows of Bramfield's Bookshop.

The fact that Carlos suggested going inside had no significance, Sophie knew. What collector would pass by a bookshop?

Mr. Bramfield was not on the premises, and the woman in charge was not someone Sophie knew well.

"Where's the travel section?" asked Carlos.

"Downstairs in the basement. I'll show you." Sophie led the way.

Presently, watching him scanning the shelves, she knew it was absurd to expect him to remember what had happened in this place four years ago. There must be scores of bookshops with similar dim, dusty basements. And how many men would remember carelessly kissing a schoolgirl even a week later?

He straightened from crouching to look at the lowest shelves. "No, I don't think there's anything here for me. What about you?"

"My hunting ground is upstairs."

As she reached the end of the narrow aisle, he touched her on the shoulder. "This isn't the first time we've been here together, is it, Sophie?"

She turned. "You *do* remember."

"It took me some time to work it out. You were only a kid then. But even in Barcelona there was something about you ... I thought I must be imagining it. It was the night I fetched you back from Nerja that at last I remembered this place, and realised that you had remembered me from the beginning. As soon as I understood that, it clarified a lot which had puzzled me."

"For example?"

"For one thing, it made some sense of the contrast between your forthcomingness in Barcelona, and your hostile manner later on. Knowing how young girls romanticise things, I came to the conclusion that you had expected me to remember you as clearly as you remembered me."

"Yes, I did," she admitted. "And when you sent me that vast basket of carnations and a poem, it seemed to confirm that idea. You must admit that any girl reading that poem would have had her head turned a little bit."

"Mm, that was a curious impulse on my part. But I didn't know at the time that you would be able to translate it, and

183

would take it literally."

"I don't suppose I should if it *had* been the first time I'd met you. But, you see, for such a long time I'd dreamed of us meeting *again* that my common sense just wasn't operating."

He undid the clasp which held her hair back from her face. "I remember your hair was like this, and you blushed and looked shocked. You were charming, but clearly too young for any follow-up."

"And a few days later you'd forgotten me!"

"Yes," he acknowledged, with a twinkle. "But not completely – and I was still free when we met again."

Sophie laughed. "This time I'll kiss you." Gently she pulled his head down.

Two weeks later they flew to the Spanish island of Menorca to stay in a low, whitewashed farmhouse which Carlos had borrowed from some friends. He had been there before and had no difficulty in finding the somewhat isolated farm. But the hired car laid on for their use was as small and hot as Sophie's car, and when they arrived he suggested that, instead of immediately unpacking, they should pause only to find their bathing kit and head for the nearest beach.

Thus it was that, within hours of her wedding, Sophie found herself lying on the fine, pink-tinged sand at Binibeca, refreshed by a bathe in water as still and transparent as a fine aquamarine. Now her wet skin was drying rapidly, and there was no sound but the muted voices of a few end-of-season holidaymakers who were bathing from the rocks by the boathouse-turned-beach-bar on the opposite side of the cove from where Carlos had spread two grass beach mats.

The past fortnight had been such a dizzying whirl of activity that Sophie still had a feeling of unreality, as if when she roused from her doze she might find it had all been a dream, and that she was back on the overcrowded shingle at Almuñecar, oppressed with troubled thoughts about the enigmatic occupant of the Moorish tower on the headland.

Sifting hot sand through her fingers, she felt the unaccustomed presence of the ring on her left hand, and sat up to look at it again, for she had not seen it till that morning. Instead of the conventional engagement ring, Carlos had given her a pair of antique Spanish crystal ear-rings. His choice of wedding ring was equally unusual. It was an Everlasting Knot made of dull yellow gold by a Ghurka regimental goldsmith. When and where he had bought it, she didn't know; but she had loved it on sight, and its heaviness suited the capable shape of her hand and her boyishly square clear-varnished nails.

Presently, their bathing suits already dry, they drove back to the farm, stopping en route for Carlos to order dinner for two at ten o'clock at a shop with a vine-shaded patio in the little village of S'Uestra.

"It may not look much of a place, but the food is excellent," he told her. "You'll need to wear a warm jersey. After dark, it becomes much cooler here."

The lane which led to the farm wound a roundabout course between the well-built dry-stone walls which also surrounded the fields and bordered the main roads. The farm itself was surrounded by hedges of tall prickly pear. On the terrace, a recent addition, bright cascades of pelargonium poured from earthenware pots. Canvas loungers invited relaxation.

"I hope Archie and Sue have remembered to organise some wine for us. If not, we shall have to run over to the bodega at San Luis," said Carlos.

But in the kitchen they found two wicker-cased, four-litre flagons, one of *blanco* and one of *tinto*, and a bottle of Carlos's favourite brandy.

"Someone's also provided some olives ... and bread ... and *chorizo*," announced Sophie, exploring a cupboard.

"A banquet," Carlos said softly.

Catching his eye, she knew he was remembering a conversation between them at Torre del Moro.

They took the wine and the olives on to the terrace, where they pulled the loungers close together, and lay holding hands and eating the juicy black fruit and drinking the cheap, good red wine. The sun was still warm, but it was sinking. In half an hour's time, perhaps less, it would leave the terrace in shadow. And then, Sophie knew, Carlos would lead her indoors, and close the bleached emerald shutters and lock out the world until it was time to go to S'Uestra for supper.

Perhaps she ought to feel shy, but somehow she didn't. Nothing about this honeymoon was as she had imagined her honeymoon. There was no bridal suite, and no balcony, and no view. There were no formal clothes in their luggage; only cotton beach clothes and books. Perhaps on the other kind of honeymoon she might have felt shy, and even nervous. As things were, she felt only the same tingling sense of anticipation which she had experienced in Barcelona the first time Carlos had smiled at her through a gap in the crowd of heads at Mrs. Hackenbacker's party.

"Why are you smiling?" he asked her.

"Was I? I was thinking about Mrs. Hackenbacker's terrible party. It was everything I most dislike, and then you appeared and left ... I felt like a bud which suddenly burst into flower."

"A flower with some mighty sharp thorns," her husband said dryly. He sat up and stroked her bare arm. "Are you beginning to feel cold? Shall we go in?"

"Yes, perhaps we should. It isn't as warm as it was out here."

As she rose, he swung her into his arm. "What you need is first a hot shower, and then a siesta, and then we'll go out and share another *paella*."

With the easy strength which had once surprised her, he carried her inside the house and shouldered the door shut.

FREE! Harlequin Romance Catalogue

Here is a wonderful opportunity to read many of the Harlequin Romances you may have missed.

The HARLEQUIN ROMANCE CATALOGUE lists hundreds of titles which possibly are no longer available at your local bookseller. To receive your copy, just 'fill out the coupon below, mail it to us, and we'll rush your catalogue to you!

Following this page you'll find a sampling of a few of the Harlequin Romances listed in the catalogue. Should you wish to order any of these immediately, kindly check the titles desired and mail with coupon.

Have You Missed Any of These
Harlequin Romances?

All books are 60c. Please use the handy order coupon.

Y

Golden Harlequin $1.95 per vol.
Each Volume Contains 3 Complete Harlequin Romances

☐ # Volume 13

DEAR SIR by Mary Burchell (No. 605)
Alexa found herself very attracted to Christopher, and she hoped with all her heart that he would never recall their first meeting. Then, quite suddenly he asked her "Were you ever in Paris?" . . . . so, he had remembered after all.

NURSE AT RYEMINSTER by Ivy Ferrari (No. 874)
Jenny Carr's complete concentration was devoted entirely to catching up with the full year's training which she had lost. When Dr. David Callender appeared on the scene, her attentions became — strangely diverted . . . .

THE BLUE CARIBBEAN by Celine Conway (No. 863)
When Ann Murray, with her brother and sister visited the exquisite Bahaman Island where her husband had left her an estate, the entire white population of Farando Kay was astonished at the three love stories which sprang up from the most unpromising of beginnings!

☐ # Volume 18

MOUNTAIN CLINIC by Jean S. MacLeod (No. 638)
Elspeth's cousin Sybil found the peace of mind which she sought, in the lovely village of Grindelwald, in the Swiss Alps. When Elspeth's life touched that of a young Scots doctor, she too found serenity and contentment, the kind which only love brings . . . .

FORBIDDEN ISLAND by Sara Seale (No. 719)
Bewildered and angry, Lisa found herself virtually a prisoner of the dark, remote chieftain of a Highland clan. With each day that passed, on the little mist-encircled isle of Culoran, this gentle captivity became easier to bear.

DEAR FUGITIVE by Elizabeth Hoy (No. 573)
Susan had never considered the possibility that Iain might fall in love, not with her, but with her sister, Jan. In flower bedecked Edinburgh, at Festival time, a time of carefree delight, an "eternal triangle" is quickly taking shape . . . .

Golden Harlequin $1.95 per vol.

Each Volume Contains 3 Complete Harlequin Romances

☐ ## Volume 23

A CASE IN THE ALPS by Margaret Baumann   (No. 778)
They had always fascinated her, and when the Rilburton family welcomed Katrina into their close-knit and charmed circle, she felt closer to them than ever — Then, she realized, that something was terribly wrong!

THE KEEPERS HOUSE by Jane Fraser   (No. 848)
Amabel was resentful that she had to leave her beloved old home and live in a small house on the estate. And even more so, when the new tenant of Kilgenny arrived — a brash young Canadian farmer — this was unbearable!

COME BLOSSOM-TIME, MY LOVE by Essie Summers   (No. 742)
Jeannie, her young brother and sister, had escaped a cruel stepfather, and come to the rich farm in New Zealand, where at last, they were happy. Affection was growing too, between Jeannie and her farm manager, until the beautiful, unscrupulous Cecily Chalmers turned up!

☐ ## Volume 28

CITY OF DREAMS by Elizabeth Hoy   (No. 542)
Three months in a real Venetian palazzo, working for a real Italian Contessa, and, in the company of Piers Mallory, her most admired Artist! Julie was so excited, but on arrival, she found things quite different . . . not at all as she had expected!

DANGEROUS OBSESSION by Jean S. MacLeod   (No. 651)
Faith's fascination for Dr. Maribeau's reputation was so great, that she married him. His insane jealousy soon spoiled their brief happiness, and drove them to exile — then, Grantland Orsett entered Faith's lonely life, only to fan the flame of the Doctor's jealousy yet again!

UNTIL WE MET by Anne Weale   (No. 855)
The highly successful star of Parisian cabaret was really, Joanna Allen an ordinary English girl, who longed to settle down and be loved, in her own home. But how could she convince the man she cared for that this was really all that mattered?